Dear Pearl,

Hope y[...] GW00391136

THE MYSTERY OF THE
MISSING FUR

To lots of
exciting adventures
with the animals!
Love
Nicole
xxx

THE MYSTERY OF THE MISSING FUR

(And Far More Mysterious Mysteries)

MICHELE SHELDON

Beastling Publishing

To my very own wonderful hairless monkeys and to all the amazing creatures in the world.

"They smashed up things and creatures and then retreated back into their money or their vast carelessness, or whatever it was that kept them together, and let other people clean up the mess they had made."
The Great Gatsby, F. Scott Fitzgerald.

With thanks to the very talented Lisa Supple for designing the cover.

First Printing, 2021, Beastling Publishing.
ISBN 978-1-8384655-0-6

Cover design by Lisa Supple @manor_mutts

Chapter 1

Bernard stood before the gates of Fluffingdale Farm and re-read his handmade posters for what seemed the millionth time that day.

Do you think Sundays are BORING?

Do you like MONKEYS?

Do you dare to be DAZZLED and AMAZED?

If it's a YES to all these questions then come and see the world's REREST monkeys perform their INCREDABLE, BREFTAKING and DEAF-DEFYING act at Fluffingdale Farm on Sunday, May 1st at 1pm. Just £1 entry! It's a WORLD PREMIHAIR!

Bernard squinted and moved his head from side to side, trying to make his drawings of Titus, Emile and Zola look less like squirrels on fire and more like monkeys performing amazing acrobatics.

And yes, his dodgy spelling had been pointed out many times. But, at least, all the information was there. People would be stupid not to come, thought Bernard.

He glanced at his watch and felt his stomach drop as a series of hideous thoughts ganged up on him and they were these:

Perhaps people did love Sundays.

Perhaps people hated monkeys.

Perhaps the people who loved Sundays and hated monkeys were at this very moment practicing strange monkey-hating ceremonies.

Because with just five minutes to go, the only people who'd turned up were:

1. A grumpy ice cream van man, hoping to make a fat profit from the crowds.
2. A reporter from the *Fluffingdale Star* who'd got the time wrong and had turned up an hour early.
3. A cyclist with a flat tyre.
4. Brenda, who didn't really count because she was meant to be here after offering to make the teas.

Bernard looked up at the sky. He at least expected to see dark grey rain clouds gathering to explain why no-one had come. But a clear blue sky gazed back down at him.

'Where is everyone?'

Even Ryan and Bob hadn't bothered to turn up and they turned up to everything, even the Onion Growers' Society's Annual General Meeting.

He gnawed at his nails watching Emile, Zola and Titus weaving in and out of the iron railings of the gate, trying to catch each other's tails.

He thought of all the time he'd spent designing posters and leaflets to advertise the show, while the monkeys had helped to bring them to life with the colours of the Brazilian flag; green, yellow and dark blue. They'd then spent a day plastering the posters all over Fluffingdale's lampposts while

Brenda badgered every customer in her village shop to take a handful of leaflets to give away.

He'd also contacted all the local TV and radio stations and newspapers, repeating the story of how he'd found the monkeys and how like him, they'd been orphanised.

Not to mention all the time they'd spent inventing a routine from all the break dancing, hip-hop moves and double and triple flips they'd already picked up from their favourite TV programme *Fame Me!*

As May was nearly upon them and the weather was turning fine, Ryan had helped Bernard transform the playground and tree house into a performance area and added five extra rope and tyre swings.

While the monkeys spent all day practising their act, Brenda taught Bernard to sew sequins and sparkles onto the monkeys' leotards. And in the evening Zola practiced playing her brand new lightweight keyboard, which would deliver the spectacular finale to their act.

'All for nothing,' he said, sulkily kicking at the gravel.

Bernard glanced down the road yet again, straining his ears desperately hoping to hear the growl of an engine approaching. Apart from a particularly keen blackbird chirping away, he could just make out a buzzing. It was either a helicopter in the distance or a large bee nearby, thought Bernard, though he couldn't be bothered to discover which.

'What more do they want? Floating bunnies? Tap dancing guinea pigs?' he said to Titus, Zola and Emile. 'Well, I'm terribly sorry the amazing hairless monkeys are so boring.'

He turned his back on them and whistled. Titus and Emile sprang onto a shoulder each and Zola took his hand. They

own the long drive towards the house where
tell the reporter and the grumpy ice cream seller
sorry but their journeys had been wasted.

make matters worse, the monkeys' chattering had grown to an ear piercing level and they began to jump up and down on his shoulders. It was something Bernard found even more annoying than their habit of leaving banana skins everywhere.

'Will you stop doing that,' said Bernard irritably. 'And you can stop being so pinchy!' he added, snatching his hand away from Zola, who had just dug her fingers into his leg.

He felt another sharp pinch and glared at Zola, who was pointing up at the horizon where a white helicopter flew towards them. He held his hand up to shield his eyes from the sun, wondering whether it was a police or hospital helicopter on the way to an emergency. There was some lettering on its side but it was too far away to read. Then the helicopter hovered over the farm before descending like a giant angry wasp.

The noise was so deafening that Bernard gathered the monkeys to him, shielding them as they watched it scoot over the house and land in the field next door. He crouched lower, terrified the wind created by its propellers may blow him and the monkeys away as easily as the pink cherry blossom now swirling through the air. With the monkeys clinging to his chest, he began walking backwards towards the house but after a few yards, he felt himself crashing into something solid.

'Woah!' said a familiar voice.

'Brenda!' he said helping her back to her feet.

They clung on to one another, waiting for the helicopter's blades to slow until they could hear themselves speak.

'The helicopter belongs to a news channel, Bernard,' shouted Brenda.

'What? Has something bad happened to Ryan?'

'No, he and Bob are fine, though very cross, by the sounds of it. They're stuck in a massive traffic jam. There's so many people on the roads coming to see the show they've jammed the tiny lanes around Fluffingdale which is why they've sent a helicopter.'

***

To say the show was a success would be like saying liquorice flyers and giant strawberry chews are quite nice. It was amazing, brilliant and triumphant. It was better than everything Bernard had promised on the poster - even if it had started two hours late because they'd had to wait for all the traffic to clear.

Bernard couldn't believe that 632 people, nine dogs and a ferret had turned up to see the show. He could only find 22 chairs so most of the audience had to stand. He and Brenda had seated all the children on the grass while the adults stood behind them so that everyone had a chance to see.

When the performance began, Bernard couldn't bear to watch. He hid round the side of the house, peeking round the corner every now and then to gauge the audience's reaction. But he didn't need to see. He could hear gasps and cheers as the monkeys jumped from one trapeze to another, performing their perfect double and triple flips.

His heart filled with pride as he remembered the days when he'd first taught them to climb and swing as babies. He'd assumed monkeys just knew how to climb and was shocked when he'd first taken them to his tree house. He expected them to jump up and start climbing straight away but they'd stared blankly at the tyre swing he'd dangled in front of them as if it was a boring bit of furniture.

It was only when he checked his copy of *Everything You Need to Know About Hairless Monkeys* that he realised they didn't know how to climb and swing because no-one had taught them how to. You see, their mother had been denied the chance to teach them because her life had been snatched away by a short-sighted trophy hunter who had mistaken her for a jaguar. Bernard had started them off on his little tree house. But before long, he'd forced himself to get over his fear of heights, helping them swing from the branches of the stumpy apple trees in the orchard. Then they'd graduated onto the giant conker tree where he hooked up a large net between the branches and watched from below as the monkeys practiced swinging and climbing for the recommended three hours a day, until they'd become the expert climbers they were born to be.

The applause and cheers snapped Bernard back to the present and he peeked around the corner in time to see the grand finale. He marvelled at the monkeys, unable to stop the smile tugging at the corners of his mouth, stretching into a massive grin. There was no doubt about it: Emile, Zola and Titus were more graceful than any ballet dancer, more flexible than any Olympic gymnast, and more bouncy than the world's bounciest ball. He watched in awe as Emile jumped onto Titus's shoulders and pulled Zola on top of his own, keyboard and all. Zola then balanced the keyboard on Emile's head and the crowd (well, mostly parents and grandparents who remembered the song) sang along to her version of *Queen's Bo-*

hemian Rhapsody at the end of which Zola somersaulted to the ground, skilfully catching the keyboard spinning in the air behind her.

Chapter 2

That evening, after Emile, Zola and Titus crashed into bed, exhausted by the day's events, Bernard dragged the sack full of 632 one pound coins into his parent's old study and locked the door.

He took a crumpled sheet of paper from his pocket, straightened it out and felt his whole body turn to ice as he took in the thin black spidery handwriting. It still had the same effect on him as it did all those years ago when it brought him official news after his parents' deaths. Now the same menacing hand was threatening to turn his and the monkeys' world upside down. Bernard gulped as he read the name at the top of the page.

Grubey and Froffit
Shark Square
London
W1
Dear Bernard,
A quick reminder that you have spent most of your inheritance and are down to your last £10,000. Please spend it wisely.
Yours,
Mr Grubey
PS: It's actually £9,800 after writing this letter.

PPS: Maybe it's time to put the house and the farm on the market? We would be more than happy to arrange a quick cash sale in its current condition.

'Yes, and maybe I'll become a money-grabbing lawyer. Not,' said Bernard, screwing the letter into a ball and throwing it across the room.

It bounced off a portrait of a red whiskered man and landed back at his feet. Bernard sheepishly looked up at his grandfather who peered back at him disapprovingly. He could almost hear him whispering: 'It's no more than you deserve after what you did.'

Turning his back on his grandfather, he heaved the sack of coins from the day's performance into the middle of the study and, with much grunting and groaning, turned it upside down. The coins flowed into a sparkling heap and Bernard was suddenly seized with the idea of rolling around in it, though gave up after a few seconds as the edges of the coins dug into his bones.

Anyway, he realised, he wasn't really rolling in money. Anything but. The monkeys performance had been an experiment to see if they could make money. If they could stand on their own two feet, or rather eight feet. And okay, they'd been successful but how long would it last for? Was it a one off? Would people really come and pay to see the monkeys perform again and again? Money was all a bit of mystery to him because he'd never ever had to worry about it before. He'd just assumed that money would always be there like, well, his hands and feet.

He sat at his father's desk and took out a piece of paper from the top drawer.

At the top in red capital letters he wrote:

MONKEY MONEY

And underneath:

£9,800 inhairitans + £632 from show = £10,432.

He looked up at his grandfather again, imagining him shaking his head in despair.

He'd be lucky if the money would last them six months. And that's only if they cut out tinned asparagus, coconut milk and sweets. And turned off the heating. And the lights. And all electrical appliances. If he didn't start earning a regular income, he would end up playing right into the money-grabbing lawyers' hands: he'd be forced to sell the farm which had been in the family for five generations.

Bernard glanced around the room and winced. He hated to admit it but Grubey and Froffit were right. Bernard saw how green mould on the walls of the office gave the blue flowers on the wallpaper a 3-D effect, how the once white ceiling was decorated with yellow stains from where the water leaked in whenever it rained and huge cobwebs hung down like mini versions of the monkeys' own trapeze swings.

He'd been so happily engrossed in bringing up the monkeys and reading about anteaters that he hadn't noticed the gradual deterioration of the house. Walls and ceilings were smeared with the monkeys' grubby fingerprints not to mention their favourite treats – asparagus, banana milkshake, coconut milk and rainbow sherbet. Beautiful silk curtains had been ripped down and fashioned into makeshift camps, while curious fingers poked holes through the family tapestries. They'd also pulled stuffing out of the sofas and chairs and the feathers out of duvets and pillows. The once manicured lawns had overgrown into meadows, the flowerbeds invaded by weeds.

He glanced up at his grandfather again and across to the mantelpiece where, long ago, he'd turned all the photos of his mother and father to face the wall and felt his gut twisting in shame.

Unless...

Bernard quickly calculated that if Emile, Zola and Titus performed three times a week to 500 people at a time, and he put the price up to £2 each, then they could make £3,000 a week. Then he'd be able to hang onto the house and the farm.

He'd shown no-one the letter, not even Brenda or Ryan because he didn't want them to worry. In fact, it had been Ryan's idea to get people to pay to see the monkeys as they were such natural show offs.

But would the monkeys be happy performing so often? They weren't even two yet and were just out of nappies. He looked across at the mantelpiece again, trying to block out the last memories of his parents angrily shouting at him. He remembered how they'd campaigned against circuses using lions and tigers. How they'd been on their last ever family holiday in a little village in France and had come across a circus in the village square where they were keeping three beautiful lions in a tiny cage called a beast wagon.

'They don't even get them in the ring, Bernard,' she'd explained. 'They just leave them in these beast wagons all day and night to attract customers.'

The house they were staying in was just around the corner and Bernard fell asleep that night listening to the lions crying pitifully in their miniature prison. When he woke the next morning, his father hurried him out of the house to the village square where his mother had handcuffed herself to the beast wagon. Bernard had felt a mixture of pride and embarrassment as the angry circus owner, a stout man with black-furred fingers, tried to saw through the handcuffs as two smiling police officers held his mother still and the lions looked on, unimpressed.

His mother had explained it was wrong to make the lions live in such a small trailer where there was barely enough room to swing a cat, let alone allow three fully grown lions to stand or turn around. They were being exploited, she said, which she explained later was a posh word for using somebody in a bad way, so that one person gets all the benefit and the other gets nothing but hardship.

Would he also be guilty of exploiting animals if he kept making the monkeys perform for money?

His eyes fell on a photo of the monkeys as babies. Brenda had taken it of him and the monkeys when he'd first brought them home from the Amazon. He couldn't believe the pathetic bald creatures pictured in his arms were the same ones who'd performed so wonderfully. They looked nothing like their baby selves. For a start their name, hairless monkey, was misleading.

Titus, named after a Roman emperor, now had a thick clump of brown hair on the top of his head which made him look as though he was a sailor at sea, the wind constantly blowing it upwards. His brother, Emile, and sister, Zola (named after Bernard's mother's favourite writer Emile Zola) had also sprouted various patches of fur. Emile was small and wiry with a long hairy ginger tail and back and a mouthful of gappy teeth, while Zola was the hairiest of the hairless monkeys with a ginger Mohican running from the top of her head down to the tip of her tail. She was between the two in size, long-limbed with dark brown eyes that always looked close to tears as if they could never forget witnessing her mother's death. While her brothers were more athletic, Zola proved to have an excellent ear for music, copying everything she heard from chart music to Mozart on Bernard's father's grand piano.

Was he as bad as the horrid beast wagon owner? Was he taking advantage of the Emile, Zola and Titus? He knew they'd do anything for him and he for them. But was that exploitation? He picked up the ball of paper at his feet and re-scrunched it into his fist. They had no other choice. Whether or not it was exploitation, the monkeys' shows were the only thing that would save them from losing their home.

Chapter 3: Three months later

'I surrender,' whimpered Bernard as he watched the three swords hover a hair's breadth from his tummy.

Another few seconds and he'd feel the cold steel tips piercing his skin before ripping through his insides.

He lay on his back, panting, fist clenched around his sword handle. He looked up at his three attackers bearing down on him. Although their faces were masked in black balaclavas, he knew they were grinning, enjoying his humiliation.

He'd taught them well. Too well. And now they'd repaid his kindness by ambushing him on the stairs. On his way back from the toilet. On his 11th birthday. How dare they. He tightened his grip on his sword handle and swung the blade across the backs of his three assailants who were left sprawled across the landing.

'Losers!' shouted Bernard as he jumped onto the shiny wooden banister and slid down to the next floor.

He glanced behind him. Two of them were still picking themselves up from the floor slightly dazed, but one of his attackers was whizzing down behind him, wielding his sword above his head. Bernard leapt on to the first floor landing and was just about to jump onto the next banister when he saw a flash of ginger fur somersaulting through the air straight for him.

'Nooooooo!'

Bernard launched himself onto the next banister to avoid the attack. As he sped down, the ball of limbs changed direction and two long arms and a tail gracefully unfurled themselves to grab hold of the huge chandelier hanging in the hallway. The tiny pieces of delicate crystal jangled softly, and then, violently, as the other two assailants flew through the air and landed on it too.

'Get down from there!' Bernard commanded, imagining the ancient chandelier crashing to the floor.

But all three ignored him. They were too busy peering out of the window at the red van heading down the driveway.

'Aha! My rescuer has come! You will be defeated,' said Bernard catching sight of the vehicle.

He ran down the rest of the stairs into the hallway towards the door but it was too late. They'd spotted him and doubled flipped off the chandelier in perfect harmony landing on Bernard's back in a whirl of monkey limbs and tails. His foam sword bounced to the floor. He pulled two of them off and threw them clear. But the smallest one had its legs and tail coiled around his neck like a snake and he felt himself becoming lightheaded as the monkey noose tightened and squeezed his throat. As he pinched at the leg, his attacker loosened her grip, but then punched Bernard's nose before slapping her little hands over his eyes. He stumbled around the hallway blindly, aware of the van door opening and slamming shut.

'Heeeelp,' he gasped.

Lurching towards the sound of the heavy footsteps on the gravel, Bernard overestimated the distance.

THWACK.

His head smacked straight into the door. For a few seconds Bernard tried to keep his balance and wondered where he was. It felt like he was floating in space. All blackness and silver stars and then... CRASH.

He opened his eyes in time to see the huge letterbox's metal lips spewing an endless stream of colourful envelopes over him, eventually followed by the sound of footsteps walking away.

'Happy birthday everyone,' he croaked as the last envelope dropped onto his forehead.

Bernard remained on the floor buried by the envelopes. He was enjoying the coldness of the ancient flagstones on his hot sweaty back and moved one envelope hiding his eyes so he could glance at the huge grandfather clock opposite. It was nearly 2pm.

They'd been sword fighting for over an hour. No wonder he was exhausted. He nervously glanced around him, worried that the monkeys were hiding and would pounce any moment. But the house was eerily silent except for the solid tick-tock of the clock. Bernard guessed they were probably resting outside in the tree house.

'Cowards,' he groaned as his fingers traced the bump of an egg-shaped bruise on his forehead.

Bernard shook himself free from his paper tomb, searching through all the envelopes for his name. But as he sorted them into two piles – one for him and one for the monkeys - he realised that all of them, except three, were addressed to Emile, Zola and Titus. He shrugged.

What did he expect? Ever since highlights of their first performance had been broadcast on *News 24*, their shows were sold out weeks ahead. The monkeys now had their own social media channel, showing videos of their performances. And they even had an Official Hairless Monkey fan page, as well as an Unofficial Hairless Monkey fan page, both run by two teenagers who'd fallen out over a packet of custard creams.

Every day the postman delivered piles of fan mail and packages containing dried coconut milk, bananas and asparagus in various stages of decay. And as today was the triplet's birthdays, it should be no surprise that they were bombarded with hundreds of birthday wishes. Though, for all Bernard knew, their birthdays could be the same as yours, reader: the day after tomorrow or Christmas Day. They could take their pick. He had no idea when their actual birthday fell. He couldn't exactly ask them, and, anyway, if they could talk, they'd hardly be able to know. So Bernard had very generously decided to share his birthday with him them; a decision he now regretted as he surveyed the paltry number of cards addressed to him. He took the first and ripped open the red envelope to reveal an image of a mouth-watering chocolate cake. Inside it read:

Happy 11th birthday, Bernard. Hope your cake turns out as good as this one!

Love Brenda xxx

He glanced behind into the kitchen at a misshapen lump standing on the sideboard and back at the perfect cake pictured. His was only recognisable as a birthday cake by the eleven wonky red and the six green candles poking out of the asparagus-flavoured butter icing. Not to everyone's taste, Bernard realised, but then not everyone shared their birthday with three Amazonian hairless monkeys celebrating their second birthdays.

Next he opened the blue envelope. Inside was a card with an illustration of a grey haired man playing golf. Shiny gold letters exclaimed *Happy birthday, Grandad!* Except the sender had tried to cross the word 'Grandad' out with pencil. But not very well.

Happy birthday, Bernard!
Yours, Ryan and Bob.

Bernard smiled. It was a slight improvement on the card they'd sent last year of a cartoon baby sucking on a dummy with a big zero scrawled next to a glittery pink number one. He lay the cards next to him, and studied the handwriting on the purple one. The sender had tried to disguise it by making it teeny-tiny.

'Brenda,' he tutted, though secretly he was pleased to receive another card.

He ripped it open to see a photo of a pygmy anteater balancing on a twig whilst gazing dreamily into the distance.

'An excellent choice,' said Bernard, grateful that Brenda had been so thoughtful.

He marvelled at the famously shy miniature anteater, who lived many thousands of miles away in the tropical forests of Central and South America and read the message inside:

Happy birthday, Bernard and happy second birthday to us!
Love Emile, Zola and Titus.

PS: Have you seen the film, The Giant Anteater? Critics have described it as an epic sweeping tale! (Get it?)

'Boom, boom,' groaned Bernard, rolling his eyes to the ceiling, and, as he did so, he glimpsed a white envelope hanging out of the corner of the letterbox as if it was sticking out its tongue at him.

He reached up, snatched the envelope and was about to toss it onto the monkeys' pile when he saw his name and address printed in a plain serious font that conjured up images of grown-ups in stuffy, silent offices, hunched over desks and computers. He wondered if it was yet another bill waiting to be paid. But, as he examined it, he decided the envelope was too heavy and expensive looking for a bill and anyway, it had a London postmark.

'Ah-ha,' smiled Bernard. 'Another pretend birthday card from the monkeys via Brenda.'

He turned the envelope over one more time as if his fingers would magically tell who had sent it before he tore it open, his stomach crashing to the flagstones as he took in the name at the top of the page.

Grubey and Froffit
Shark Square
London
W1
Dear Bernard,
Happy 11th birthday!
Yours, Mr Grubey and Mr Froffit.
PS: Just another friendly reminder that you are very close to having no money whatsoever - £9,800.
PPS: Well, actually £9,600 after writing this letter.
PPPS: Me and Mrs Grubey would be happy to make an offer on the house and farm.

'£200 to wish me happy birthday!' shouted Bernard. 'Why don't you just leave us alone?'

He scrunched the letter into a ball and threw it along the corridor, sending a herd of dust balls scuttling across the hallway as if they were fleeing Bernard's ill temper.

The monkeys had earned enough to see them through the winter but in a couple of months they would need to break into the last of his inheritance. He had tried to keep their impending money shortage to the back of his mind. Life had been good until *Grubey and Froffit* had reminded him they may soon find themselves on the streets any time soon.

What chance did he, an 11-year-old boy, have against two fully grown adult lawyers?

Bernard tried to conjure up various fanciful solutions, mostly involving winning large amounts of money, or digging up a pot of fabulously rare golden coins but none remained a solution for longer than a few seconds.

So, instead, like many excellent avoiders of trouble, he decided to bury his head in the sand. Except in Bernard's case, the sand was the huge pile of birthday cards from the monkeys' fans, though he found little comfort from their many words of love.

Chapter 4

The sound of wheels crunching on the driveway brought Bernard out of his stupor. His head emerged from the pile of cards like a tortoise from its shell and he dragged himself to the hall window. They weren't expecting any guests until late afternoon when Brenda, Ryan and Bob were coming for a birthday tea.

As he peered along the driveway, he caught sight of a very shiny blue car coming slowly towards the house.

'Woah! A Bentley!' said Bernard, recognising its famous winged motif on the front of the car. 'They must be lost,' he muttered to himself. 'Unless Brenda has finally won the Lottery?' he wondered, thinking, for a split second, that perhaps the chances of winning a large amount of money to solve his financial worries wasn't out of the question after all.

He opened the door just as Emile, Zola and Titus came racing in from the garden. They jumped on Bernard's back and together they watched the car slow to a halt next to them. Bernard peered through the blacked out windows, hoping to catch sight of the passengers but his own distorted reflection, adorned with three monkey heads, peered back.

The driver's door opened and a short wiry man dressed in a chauffeur's hat and suit got out and walked to the back passenger seat. Bernard felt his eyes popping out of his head as a giant ginger quiff emerged through the door, followed by its owner: a tall, thin man dressed in a purple shiny suit and pointy black shoes which crunched their way over the gravel to the front door.

'Sebastian Trophy-Assetclass?' said Bernard, wondering what on earth the host of the massively popular TV reality show *Fame Me!* was doing in Fluffingdale on a Sunday afternoon, or in fact, on any afternoon.

The sight of the famous star took Bernard back to when he was five or six years old. Sebastian Trophy-Assetclass had been his idol, performing the incredible floating bunny act where dozens of rabbits, dressed in superhero capes, flew around the stage.

'It can't be,' Bernard whispered as the monkeys jumped down and gripped his legs.

They looked at one another and then at Bernard who was still lost in a daze. As well as making people stars, Sebastian Trophy-Assetclass was famous for his shock of ginger hair which was used to promote a leading brand of shampoo. And as Bernard and the three monkeys stared open-mouthed at him, they could see why the media loved to comment about it so much. It sat on his head like a separate being, almost like a comet blazing across the watery blue sky.

Titus quickly ran his hands though his own quiff, as if embarrassed by its lack of quiffiness in the presence of a quiff-tastic legend, while Emile and Zola stood behind Bernard, peaking up at the mega-celebrity. As Sebastian turned to them, he smiled such a dazzling whiter than white smile, it made Bernard wobble slightly.

'I'm going to fame you, you and you!' announced Sebastian, pointing to each of the monkeys with a perfectly manicured finger.

It was only when he removed his huge sunglasses and turned his famous tiger eyes on them that Bernard felt a flicker of something unpleasant pass over him. He couldn't quite put his finger on why. But it was the same feeling you get when you're really looking forward to eating some delicious-looking sweets or chocolates, and somehow, they don't taste as great as you expected. And, sometimes, they leave a very nasty taste in your mouth.

Chapter 5

Over the following weeks, Bernard felt as though he was in one of those snow globes you get at Christmas. You know the ones with Santa and his reindeers flying over a beautifully snowy landscape? Except the scene was Bernard and the monkeys snuggled up next to the fireside reading their favourite Mr Wolf picture book. And that someone (namely Sebastian Trophy-Assetclass) had shaken it violently and left the globe turned upside down for good. Accidently on purpose.

But while Bernard floundered around trying to make sense of their rapid change in fortune, Titus, Emile and Zola went happily along with whatever Sebastian asked of them. Far too happily for Bernard's liking. He could feel the knots forming in his tummy every time they ran to the door to greet Sebastian, and his chauffeur, who was always laden down with presents for the monkeys.

A quick word here, reader. You see, jealousy was as alien to Bernard as well, an alien. He'd never before had any reason to be jealous of anyone in his whole life. He had no siblings, and therefore no rivals for his parent's affection, and he'd always had everything he'd ever wanted in terms of material things. Of course, he'd felt envious of other people with families ever since being orphanised.

But jealousy was another thing all together. It lay uncomfortably in the pit of his tummy like a heavy meal of greasy chips and sausages. Night and day it whispered bad thoughts, and during the odd occasions when he happened to glance in the mirror, he noticed it had pulled his features into someone he no longer recognised, let alone liked the look of.

So, when the day arrived for Bernard to sign a year's contract for the monkeys to appear on the hit TV show *Fame Me!*, he was tempted to scribble all over it, rip it up into tiny pieces and shower them all over Sebastian's stupid quiff. But, as he looked at the monkeys' eyes wide in excitement, and more to the point, the thought of the large guaranteed payment he'd receive every month, keeping *Grubey and Froffit* from the door, he went ahead and signed, knowing full well he'd just destroyed the happy world he'd created.

***

One week later, Bernard said goodbye to Titus, Emile and Zola.

Sebastian had hired the best choreographer in the world, who was flying over from Los Angeles, and their work schedule meant they'd have to stay in London all week and could only come home at weekends.

'I know it must be hard for you, Bernie, letting go like this. But you've got to let them follow their dreams,' said Sebastian, patting his head.

'It's Bernard. Not Bernie,' mumbled Bernard as he followed Sebastian to the front door.

'Not to worry, Bernie. I love monkeys! I'll treat them as my own babies,' said Sebastian, hurrying towards his Bentley.

I'd rather you didn't, thought Bernard. Although Sebastian had been his childhood hero, Bernard couldn't see anything remotely heroic about him now he was getting to know him.

In fact, despite desperately wanting to like Sebastian, Bernard now found himself repulsed by his famous quiff and strangely waxy unlined skin.

As the chauffeur opened the door to the car, Bernard saw that the back seat was now covered in thick plastic.

'You do know they're toilet trained,' said Bernard.

'Yes, but I don't want them secreting their oils over my car seats, thank you,' Sebastian sneered.

'Oils?' said Bernard, puzzled. 'But they don't secrete oils...'

'Everyone secretes oils, Bernie.'

'It's Bernard,' snapped Bernard and was about to add that he certainly didn't secrete any oil when he saw the chauffeur open the boot and bring out a large metal cage.

'Just in case they start playing up,' explained Sebastian.

'They've never been in a cage in their lives! Even when I brought them over on the plane. Anyway, they won't 'play up' if you talk to them nicely,' said Bernard.

'There's a first time for...'

'No!' said Bernard, squaring up to Sebastian. 'There's no need and if you insist on using it, they won't be going anywhere with you.'

Sebastian's tiger eyes narrowed at Bernard who'd protectively put his arms around the monkeys. Sebastian then nodded for the chauffeur to put the cage back into the boot of the car.

Bernard stormed over and snatched the cage from the

chauffeur. 'I'll look after that, thank you. And if I find out that you're using cages then our contract is broken.'

Sebastian glowered at Bernard, his waxy skin reddening, his fulsome lips twitching.

'Remember the contract works both ways,' he said glancing up at the rotten wooden window frames. 'Your house is falling to pieces, Bernard. I think it's time we say goodbye.'

The monkeys clung onto Bernard and he willed them not to let go and to change their minds. He'd always loved the feeling of their soft little hands on the back of his neck as he carried them around. It made him feel needed and loved. And now he was having to peel away their little fingers from him as if peeling away all the happiness and love they'd brought to him.

'Come on you lot! You'll see Bernard in a week's time,' said Sebastian, as his chauffeur lifted them one by one into the back of the car and shut the door.

Bernard gulped back his tears as he saw their little faces appear at the window, blowing kisses to him and chattering excitedly.

'Wait a moment!' he called.

He motioned for the chauffeur to lower the window and reached into his pockets, pulling out three small but bulging paper bags.

'Rainbow sherbet for the journey,' said Bernard, handing them a bag each as the car begin to move off down the drive.

He ran alongside, waving manically at the monkeys, pulling silly faces to keep them smiling until they reached the end of the driveway from where the car sped off down the narrow country lane.

As soon as they was out of sight, Bernard's face crumpled like an empty crisp packet being trampled by a herd of cows and he ran straight to his office where he cried non-stop for 4 hours, 30 minutes and 20 seconds.

Chapter 6

'No can do, Bernie. We're scheduled for practice all weekend,' said Sebastian during one of their twice weekly video calls.

'But you promised you'd bring them down for a visit this weekend,' said Bernard. 'I mean... they haven't been home for over a month now. Not since you took them away.'

'Hey, Bernie, that's showbusiness. I can't help being a major international celebrity who everyone wants to hang out with,' said Sebastian, running his fingers through his quiff and pouting.

Bernard wondered why being a major international celebrity had anything to do with the monkeys practising.

'Anyway, what are they practicing for? What's so important?'

Sebastian tapped a manicured finger to the side of his nose. 'Top secret, I'm afraid. I'd have to kill you if I told you,' he said matter of factly and Bernard had the feeling that Sebastian would actually quite like to kill him.

'But I want to see them. In fact, I demand to see them! They must have some free time? Why don't you drive them down during the week?'

'Watch my lips, Bernie. International celebrities do not do

driving monkeys around the countryside. All that dirt not to mention the foxes and beavers...'

'Beavers?' said Bernard, trying to work out where on earth Sebastian had seen a beaver at Fluffingdale. 'Ah, you mean badgers!' he exclaimed loudly.

Sebastian jumped out of his chair, screaming: 'Where? Where? Get them away from me!'

'No, I meant you must mean badgers instead of -'

'My god! Have you seen the size of their teeth and nails,' said Sebastian, running his hand through his quiff as if to check it was still there before sitting down again gingerly. 'You seriously expect me to put my hair at risk, Bernie?'

'I'm sure badgers aren't interested in your hair.'

Sebastian draw back in horror and turned very red before roaring: 'EVERYONE is interested in my hair.'

'If you say so,' muttered Bernard, well used to Sebastian's tantrums. 'What about your chauffeur? He could drive them,' he suggested, thinking how strange it was that Sebastian's aversion to the countryside hadn't stopped him visiting on numerous occasions to shower the monkeys with gifts and persuade Bernard to sign the contract.

'He's my driver. He drives me where I want to go to 24/7. He's not the monkeys' personal driver. He's mine. Got it?'

'Yes, but I didn't say he was their personal driver...' said Bernard, wondering why Sebastian was always so unreasonable.

'I'm an international celebrity. Can you imagine how hard my life is?'

'Um...' said Bernard. 'Not really.'

'Well, maybe you should do. Stop being so selfish and think about other people for a change. Goodbye.'

The computer screen suddenly went blank.

'Hello? Hello?' said Bernard hoping it was a dodgy internet connection but Sebastian had well and truly gone.

He tried ringing again but a notice popped up to say the line was busy.

Bernard glanced out of the window at the grey sky and wondered if it were possible for the clouds to grow any gloomier. He remembered his dad talking about black and white TV and how even beachgoers bathed under a grey sky. He realised that was exactly how his world had become. The only time a few rays of sunshine broke through was when Titus, Emile and Zola face-timed. But it'd now been a whole week since he'd spoken to them. Ryan and Bob dropped in several times to check on him and Brenda personally delivered his copy of *Anteaters Monthly* because he'd failed to pick it up from the shop, but Bernard had sent them away in a choked voice, saying he was far too busy to chat. Twice they'd managed to coax him out of his office with cakes, but even then Bernard would sit stabbing at the jammy donut or cream slice, wondering where his appetite had gone.

On the few occasions he'd managed to say hello to Titus, Emile and Zola, Bernard's heart had felt as if it were being stabbed by a thousand little knives as he watched Sebastian struggling to get the monkeys to come to the computer screen. More and more frequently, he was forced to watch Sebastian, wearing a protective gown, mask and washing up gloves, plonking them in front of the screen.

They'd smile and wave at Bernard for a few seconds, before

slinking back to their computer games on the laptops Sebastian had bought them. Bernard often sat feeling a rage burning silently inside him, a rage that would match the monkeys' subsequent tantrums as Sebastian turned off their games, made them return to a waiting Bernard where they crossed their arms and pouted sulkily, looking everywhere but at him.

Bernard tried calling again. If they couldn't travel to Fluffingdale, then he'd travel to London. But straightaway a pop up box said Sebastian was now offline.

'I hate you, Sebastian Trophy-Assetclass,' growled Bernard as he remembered what happened when he suggested he visit the week before.

The session had ended abruptly with Zola having a leg and arm-flailing tantrum because she was half-way through a computer game involving bananas, masked cats and sharp knives.

'No, I don't think that's a good idea. It's too unsettling for them,' Sebastian had spluttered. 'Anyway, I'm busy. I'm shooting a new shampoo ad,' he'd added, running his hands through his quiff.

'Well, I'll come and look after them,' offered Bernard.

'No, sorry, Bernie. No can do. They've asked to come too. They've been looking forward to it all week. We'll be down next weekend,' Sebastian had promised.

'I could come too,' Bernard had suggested feebly.

'I need my space, Bernie. Can you imagine the pressure I feel when I make a new shampoo advert knowing this,' he said pointing at his face, 'is going to be adored and worshipped by millions of people worldwide?'

'Well...'

'Next weekend. Pinky promise,' he said waving his gloved little finger in the air.

But next weekend had come and gone and now Bernard had to face the truth: the monkeys didn't care about him. They looked upon Sebastian as their new father, mother and friend.

He wiped a tear away from his cheek as he stared at the photo of him and the monkeys as babies. He thought back on the day he'd rescued them. How he'd ducked out of sight when he saw the evil trophy hunter taking a shot at the monkeys' mother. He'd try to yell out to warn her but no words had come. He'd felt as helpless then as when he'd watched his own mother and father perish.

Bernard knew the babies would die any number of horrid deaths alone in the forest. You see, ever since their births, an anaconda had been eyeing them up as a tasty snack. And the jaguar that the game hunter had tried to shoot was just as mean. He'd been monitoring the babies' growth very closely. Every morning after sharpening his claws, he would mark another line on the base of a rubber tree, counting down the days until the babies reached a perfect mouth-watering chubbiness, when he would pounce and devour the lot in one sitting.

In addition, a pink-toed tarantula living on a nearby tree had been busy plotting an elaborate plan, involving a fake moustache, nuts and coconut milk, to trap the monkeys in her huge web.

The monkeys were highly prized by all types of beasts, including the human type, because of these three facts:

1. Their meat was sweet and tender.
2. Eating them, skin and all, did not leave annoying hairs stuck between your teeth.
3. Their bones* could be ground down into fine powder to provide so-called cures for baldness and a fear of heights known as vertigo.

A note here, reader. Hairless monkey bones definitely DO NOT provide cures for baldness and vertigo just like rhino horns DO NOT make you look younger or cure you of any illnesses. The only thing that grinding their bones and horns into powder does is to kill the poor animals.

Bernard felt his face burning at the thought of the evil game hunter who'd shot their mother. Like many story book heroes, Bernard knew what it was like to be orphanised, a word he'd invented because it made him feel less tragic than the cold, stark orphaned.

He'd watched his own mother and father die in a hot air ballooning accident in Africa when he was just eight years old. Witnessing the monkey's mother being shot dead had brought back the tragedy and he'd raced to the monkeys' rescue, despite the fact that the hunter was in the middle of reloading his rifle and was about to take another shot.

Bernard couldn't bear to leave the monkeys to their deaths. If they weren't picked off by the many hungry creatures in the forest, he knew one of the trophy hunter's guides would bundle them into a sack with their mother's dead body.

He pictured their little bodies cooked, dried and ground into powder, sold for a range of quack cures in the markets of the Far East. Demand for these so-called medicines, alongside rhino horn and elephant tusks, made hairless monkeys ten times more precious than gold. What made the creatures even more desirable was that they rarely ventured below 100ft, preferring the company of clouds at the top of the largest tree in the forest, the Kapok tree. And who could blame them when the world below was so wicked?

He'd planned to hand the babies to Manaus Zoo. But after two weeks of trekking through the forest, spooning coconut milk and tinned asparagus and palm hearts into the babies' ever hungry mouths, singing *Twinkle Twinkle Little Star* every time they began to cry, and cuddling them at night to keep them warm, Bernard found he was rather attached to the monkeys and they to him. In fact, they now believed he was their mother and often worked as gang, wrestling him to the ground, trying and failing to suckle from him.

The night before he was due to deliver them to the zoo, he'd lay in his bed batting away the hot tears pouring down his cheeks. Gazing down at the babies' perfect little limbs wrapped around him, he imagined an impossible farewell and the memory of his own parents' deaths returned a hundred-fold to haunt him. He'd pictured the monkeys huddled together in the corner of a smelly damp zoo pen, pining away for him as a succession of zoo keepers tried to coax them out of their depression. He could not bear to think of them suffering as he had done with no parents to look out for them.

So, after a fretful night's sleep, he resolved to fly them home to England. He saw no better place than Fluffingdale, the 200-acre estate he'd inherited from his parents to bring them up. His motives weren't entirely altruistic. The monkeys would be his constant companions and playmates. And most importantly he had someone to love and someone to love him.

But now, thanks to Sebastian, he was alone once again.

Chapter 7: Christmas Eve

'How are those monkeys of yours getting on? Excited about Christmas, no doubt?' asked Brenda, handing him a tea towel to dry himself with.

Overnight, torrential rain and gusty storms had blown away two weeks of beautiful winter sunshine. And although Bernard had donned his wellington boots, rain cape and hat, by the time he got to the village store, he was soaked through.

'All fine, thanks, and yes...very excited,' he replied, handing her back the soggy tea towel.

'You must have missed 'em?'

'Not really,' lied Bernard, pretending to peruse the magazines on display. 'Though I suppose it has been a bit boring without them.'

'I've got presents for you and the monkeys. Maybe I could pop round this afternoon? It's early closing.'

'Well, they actually haven't arrived yet,' said Bernard, thinking back on all the dozens of calls he'd made to Sebastian trying to find out exactly what time they were arriving for Christmas.

Each time he managed to get through, Sebastian complained the line was too bad to hear anything and he was cut off. Bernard tried to ignore the niggling worry that Sebastian would let him down yet again and reached for a copy of the *Radio Times*.

'Oh, I thought they'd be with you well before Christmas...' said Brenda, pointing to a tabloid newspaper on the counter. 'Instead of gallivanting around that London with the rich and famous.'

'Sorry?' said Bernard, trying to dig his hand into his sodden pocket for some change.

'You know... all them film previews and shampoo launches with famous pop stars and film stars and the like. You can't open a newspaper these days without seeing their cheeky little faces staring up at you. And just to think I used to change their nappies!'

Bernard tried not to look too shocked. Sebastian had told him they'd been busy practising their performances, not accompanying him late at night, mixing with the rich and famous.

'You don't reckon you can get some autographs, do you? I love that Sebastian Asset Class Trophy.'

'Sebastian Trophy-Assetclass,' corrected Bernard.

Though between you and me and that far wall, ever since the missed weekends and video calls, Bernard always used his own name for him. One which involved stripping away one 's' and one 't' from the word 'asset' and adding an 'r' to rhyme with class.

'He's got beautiful hair, though not as nice as your Mr Pew's,' she said, gazing out of the window towards Fluffingdale Farm as Bernard desperately scanned the newspapers, trying to make sense of what she'd told him.

'You mean, Ryan?'

'Oh yes, that Ryan of yours.'

'He's not mine.'

'You know what I mean. Him and your dad were as thick as thieves as kids. Anyway, Ryan could be in a shampoo advert if he wanted to be.'

'I don't suppose Ryan would want to be in a shampoo advert,' said Bernard, wondering why on earth Brenda was so interested in Ryan's hair and its suitability for the selling of shampoo, all of a sudden.

Brenda came out of her dreamy state and pointed at the copy of *The Daily Celeb*. 'They're on page 5. It's a great picture!'

Bernard flicked through the pages until he came to the offending photo, his eyes growing as large as the giant gobstoppers for sale on the shelves. Pictured were his monkeys at a nightclub cuddling up to an elderly man with a grey mullet (a kind of hairstyle your dad or grandpa may have sported in the early 1980s, short at the top, long and straggly at the bottom. Go on. Ask to see photographic evidence.)

As much as Bernard didn't want to let Brenda know he had zero idea about what they were up to, he couldn't help himself.

'Virgil Boghero? What on earth are they doing with that slimeball?'

He grabbed the paper and read the predictable headline:

Punters go bananas for Boghero's new pals.

And then the picture caption:

Fourth night out in a row for Sebastian's protégés Ding,

Dang and Dong at the opening of his best friend's new night-club, Snazzle Dazzle.

'Ding, Dang and Dong? Sebastian's protégées?' Bernard exploded as the little knives stabbed repeatedly at his heart again. 'HOW DARE HE CHANGE THEIR NAMES!'

'Oh, Bernard, love. I thought you knew. I thought they were just their stage names to give them a bit of you know...glamour, a bit of razzmatazz...'

'Ahhhh,   rrrrrrr,   grrrrrr,   ahhhh,   gr-rrrrrrrrrrrrrrrrrrrrrrrrrrrrrrrrrrrrrrrrrr,' shouted Bernard and other difficult to spell expressions of disbelief at Sebastian's betrayal.

'Who was the one who saved them and looked after them?' he eventually spluttered.

'Oh, Bernard,' said Brenda, scuttling from behind her counter to comfort him.

He thought of all the work he'd done over the last few weeks to make this Christmas the best ever. He'd ordered the biggest Christmas tree he could find, as well as all the festive food they'd need, with lots of treats including almond and Brazil nuts, crates of bananas and huge tubs of rhubarb ice-cream, Brussel sprouts, cabbage, rainbow sherbet and, of course, a stack of tinned asparagus that stretched from floor to ceiling.

He'd also ordered all the monkeys' favourite toys; Lego *Star Wars* sets for Titus and Emile, a new keyboard and set of drums for Zola, and for all three, five marble runs that could be connected throughout the house.

As soon as the presents were delivered, he'd taken them upstairs to his room, spending hours wrapping them beautifully in bows and ribbons and hand-making each label adorned with little heartfelt or jokey messages.

He'd even built them a second tree house with Ryan's help, decked out in a thick luxurious brown carpet and wall-papered with exploding supernovas and spiral galaxies. Bernard then set about building a bridge leading to the first tree house – all for nothing by the looks of it.

'It's all right, Bernard,' said Brenda, returning behind the counter.

She took down a big jar of rhubarb and custards and quickly shovelled out a large scoop into a bag. 'You need something for the shock,' she said, opening Bernard's mouth and dropping one inside.

Bernard crunched down hard on the sweet, imagining he was crushing Sebastian's bones, grinding the shattered pieces into tiny splinters and obliterating him from the face of the earth. No wonder the monkeys hadn't visited. They were out on the town every night, entertaining pop stars and celebrities, thought Bernard. He was so angry that he could almost hear the bubbling of his blood as it boiled away in his veins.

He handed over the damp coins for his magazine, wishing Brenda a rather choked 'Merry Christmas' before walking stiffly from the shop, his limbs and heart numb from the cold and heartbreak.

Bernard stormed home unknowingly pursued by a filthy black cloud, shaped liked an old farm wagon, which halfway there dropped its load of very heavy and painful hail upon him. As he stood blinking back the icy lumps, a sleek black car slowed then raced past, its wheels hitting the deepest, dirtiest and iciest puddle in the long, long history of deepest, dirtiest and iciest puddles, throwing up a tsunami of water. The wave not only re-drenched Bernard but forced him onto the verge, where he stumbled and crashed into an overflowing, stinking ditch.

For a few moments, Bernard remained floating on his back, contemplating who could have been so mean to have driven through the giant puddle on purpose, while desperately trying to push away the image of the three familiar faces he'd glimpsed laughing at him through the steamed up car window.

Chapter 8

When Bernard returned to the house, he found Ryan sheltering from the rain in the porch with Bob, his sheepdog.

'I feel j...j...j li...li...ke you, Bob,' said Bernard, his teeth chattering, noticing how the poor dog was shaking, his tail between his legs.

Ryan leant down and stroked Bob's wet fur.

'How he feels has nothing to do with the cold,' he snapped. 'Let's just say them monkeys have lost none of their spite for Bob.'

'They're here already? Where are they?' asked Bernard, who, in his excitement, forgot to ask what Ryan was talking about.

But Ryan didn't answer. As Bernard went into the house, Bob bolted from the porch towards the Land Rover with Ryan striding after him.

'Happy Christmas!' Bernard waved, though Ryan didn't bother to turn around.

Bernard shrugged and shut the door behind him, his cape dripping a trail of water as he took in the heap of suitcases and coats dumped messily in the hallway. He whipped off his cape, trying to ignore the chill seeping into his bones and his parents' voices telling him to go and change into something dry or he'll catch his death. Because despite the damp clothes clinging to him, just knowing the monkeys were at home at last, warmed his heart.

'Zola, Emile, Titus! I'm home!' called Bernard, eagerly listening out for the sound of their little feet pitter-pattering down the stairs to greet him. 'Where are you?'

But the only reply came from the tick-tock of the grandfather clock.

'Hiding are you?' said Bernard, climbing the grand staircase before stopping mid-step as he heard giggling.

'Fee-fi-fo-fum,' he sang in his best troll voice as he carried on up the stairs, making his way towards his bedroom.

The monkeys always loved being in his room, usually to play some trick on him, either leaving a cup of water or a mouldering banana skin balanced on top of a door left ajar. However, the door was just how he'd left it. Shut. He placed his hand on the door handle, certain they were inside, behind the door or curtains, or under the bed, ready to pounce. Bernard made a series of rabid sniffing noises outside to warn them, before bursting into the room.

'Ah-ha!'

Bernard glanced around, disappointed to see it was empty.

Indeed, it was clear to Bernard by the state of his vaguely tidy and unmonkeyed-with-bedding that no-one had been there since he'd got up that morning.

They'll be in their bedroom of course, he thought. Playing with their toys.

'Fee-fi-fo-fum, I smell the blood of a monkey bum, Be they alive or be they dead, I'll grind their bones to make my bread!' sang Bernard as he checked their room.

But it too was empty as were all the other bedrooms.

He then made his way down the hallway towards the staircase and again heard giggling. This time it was clearly coming from downstairs. They must have sneaked past him while he was checking the other rooms, Bernard assumed.

'Fee-fi-fo-fum!' he started again but didn't get very far because the next thing he knew, he was slipping on a discarded banana skin and crashing down the stairs, landing at the bottom in a soggy heap.

'Ow! Ow! Ow!' he cried, waiting for the monkeys to come to his aid.

He listened out for the soft patter of their feet approaching and when he heard nothing but silence began to wail.

'OWWWWWW!'

Bernard stopped and sat for a moment, rubbing his lower back and bottom and then froze at what sounded like the tiniest floorboard squeaking. After a few moments, however, he realised that was wishful thinking. The squeaking wasn't from any floorboard, he realised, feeling tears prickling. It was the sound of the monkeys giggling.

He managed to pick himself up and limped down the long corridor, holding onto the walls for support, every and now whimpering in pain. Eventually, he stumbled into the half-closed office door, the giggling now mixed with a familiar booming voice.

'Atichooo!' he sneezed.

He poked his head around the corner and saw all three staring at his laptop. He hobbled closer, hoping the monkeys would turn to acknowledge him. But their gazes were fixed on the screen. And, as Bernard drew closer, he could see why.

Sebastian, dressed only in a mauve pair of tight swimming trunks, was taking them on a laptop tour around a luxurious mansion overlooking an impossibly calm blue sea. Next to the pool in the far corner, Bernard saw a bald pink-faced man stretched out on a sun lounger fast asleep. At his feet, lay a grey furry creature, seemingly fast asleep too. Bernard peered at it trying to work out whether it was a lap dog, a miniature dachshund, perhaps, or even a Persian cat, before his thoughts were interrupted by the man waking himself up with a loud pig-like snore. Realising he was on camera, the bald man grabbed the grey creature at his feet and plonked it over his face.

How strange, thought Bernard, who was feeling rather strange himself as he tried to focus on the man with the now obscured hairy face.

But the camera was on the move again. Sebastian was walking down some steep stairs. At the bottom, he opened a large golden door to reveal a cinema room and a girl, busily mopping the floor between the rows of seats. Her head of brown curls hid her face but Bernard could see from her size that she was probably no older than him.

'Out of the way, girl,' Bernard thought he heard Sebastian mutter, shooing her away like a stray dog.

The girl picked up her bucket of soapy water, and scuttled across to the other side of the room, but not before pulling a face and sticking her tongue out at Sebastian's back.

'No, I mean out of the room. You're ruining the view,' he snarled before turning back to the monkeys with a big smile on his face. 'You guys would love this place,' he said, zooming his laptop around to a large popcorn machine at the end of the aisle now filled with Brazil nuts.

Next to it stood a glass cabinet packed full of jars of rainbow sherbet. The monkeys leaned into the laptop and whimpered. Bernard shook his head to try and get rid of the dizzy feeling he'd had since falling down the stairs. It felt as if his head was full of glue, each thought tapering off before they had a chance to become complete. Sebastian exited the cinema and climbed back up the steps before arriving at a glistening eternity pool, merging with what looked very much like the Caribbean Sea.

'Christmas in Barbados is the best. Lots of sunshine and no boring old English rain. It's such a shame you got turned away from the airport like that,' he said.

'What?' muttered Bernard. 'Turned away at the airport?'

But he didn't have time to find out more because Sebastian was on the move again.

'And look who's here, your old mate Virgil.'

The very same Virgil Boghero who Bernard had seen draping his hideous arms around the monkeys in the newspaper just an hour before came into view, sweeping his grey dishevelled hair into a ratty pony tail.

'Hi guys,' said Virgil, prompting Titus, Emile and Zola to start crying.

'Hey, hey, hey! Ding, Dang, Dong! Next time, I'll make sure you have your passports ready in time,' said Sebastian.

'Yes, you're making us wait...' said Virgil sharply, before smiling and seemingly correcting himself. 'I mean we can't wait to see you out here.'

Virgil and Sebastian flashed their over the top white fake

teeth and waved goodbye, totally ignoring Bernard, who they must have been able to see standing in the background behind the monkeys.

But the monkeys didn't see Sebastian and Virgil's farewell because they were far too busy holding onto one another sobbing. Bernard shuffled forward and patted them on their backs gently.

'There, there. You're home now,' he said before placing his arms around the monkeys. 'You'll have lots of fun here,' he added just as Titus sharply pushed him away and he stumbled into the wall.

Bernard felt as though Titus had ripped his heart out, stamped on it and set it on fire. He turned and limped back into the corridor, slumping against the wall, his soggy back leaving a ghostly, dejected shadow.

'Turned away at the airport? Titus pushing me away?' he whispered. Surely not. I must be dreaming, he thought. This can't be happening, he convinced himself, after having imagined their heartwarming reunion for weeks.

Bernard shook his head, drops of dirty ditchwater spraying over the walls, joining all the sherbet, asparagus and coconut milk stains. I must have misheard, he told himself, and hobbled back into the office to tell the monkeys he was so happy they were home.

'Welcome home!' he said, throwing his arms out wide.

This time all three turned and threw their hands over their noses and fled the room as if Bernard had done a big stinky fart.

Chapter 9

Something to remember, reader. If you're having a bad time, don't ever make statements like: things can't get any worse. Because, as Bernard discovered, often things can get a whole lot worse. Having been rejected by the monkeys, Bernard gave himself a good sniff and quickly recoiled. He stank of mouldering rotten meat and cabbage mixed with cheesy feet and filthy public toilets. No wonder they hadn't wanted him anywhere near them.

If it was bad for him, what was it like for monkeys who had super-strength sniffing powers like anteaters, warthogs and dogs?

Bernard crawled upstairs and slowly unpeeled his wet clothes, wincing at the large red and purple bruises appearing on his hip and thighs. He staggered into the shower and afterwards, with great difficulty, changed into his pyjamas and dressing gown, all the while pushing away the image of the monkeys fleeing the room because he stank so much.

And then many darker thoughts appeared. The monkeys didn't actually like him anymore. They'd tried to go to Barbados with Sebastian. They didn't consider Fluffingdale home anymore.

Then, the memory of the monkeys laughing at him

through the car window as they drove through the giant puddle, came flooding back. I must have imagined it, he insisted. It must be someone else, evil triplets perhaps who happened to be passing and who just happened to be wearing the exact same lime green sequined shellsuits as the monkeys. And anyway, if it had been the monkeys, they must have been laughing at something else. They couldn't have possibly known it was me! I was dressed in an oversized rain cape and hat, thought Bernard. And if they had known, then surely they would have stopped to give me a ride home?

He ignored the little voice in his head that whispered: '*But Bernard, it doesn't matter if they knew it was you or not. Because they shouldn't have splashed anyone on purpose, let alone laughed about it. They should have stopped and pulled you out of the ditch and apologised.*' And then the same voice whispered something even darker: '*Perhaps you deserved to be splashed because you don't deserve to be happy ever again after what you did.*'

Bernard screwed up his face, eventually squeezing the bad thought out of his brain and limped to the sitting room to find the monkeys. They were busy playing computer games and barely glanced up as he walked in.

'Beautiful, isn't it?' he said, pointing to the giant Christmas tree dominating the room.

It was adorned with little photos of the monkeys he'd taken over the last two years and dozens of chocolate santas and reindeers, though most of the latter now lay half-eaten and squashed into the carpet.

'Zola? What do you think?' asked Bernard.

She grabbed a piece of paper and then drew a picture of a

small tree with a sad face and then a large one with a happy face. Bernard felt his chest puffing out with pride as he looked at the drawing and smiled. He'd spent hours dressing the tree and printing off the photos and mounting them on cardboard stars and now he was reaping the rewards of his hard work.

That is until Titus gestured at Bernard's Christmas tree and then pointed at the small one in his picture. He then mimed a quiff and pointed at his picture of the big tree and shook his head in disappointment.

'Happy Christmas to you too!' Bernard sniffed as he turned from the room and crawled upstairs to bed.

***

The next morning, despite Bernard's head being thick with a cold, and his muscles feeling as though they'd been run over by a convoy of bulldozers and tractors on their way to the World's Heaviest Vehicle Convention, he made it downstairs for present opening. He bit his tongue as Emile, Titus and Zola carelessly tossed the presents aside along with the paper, ribbons and bows he'd spent so long perfecting before sauntering back to their computer games.

And one of the few things he'd learnt at school came back to him. 'How sharper than a serpent's tooth it is to have a thankless child.' It was a quote from the play *King Lear* by Shakespeare. He wiped away the tears from his eyes, cringing about the times he'd been ungrateful for all the lovely things that his parents had done for him. His heart ached to have the luxury of being ungrateful to them again. If just for one moment, he could go back in time, and tell them how much he loved them. How sorry he was.

But -

After cooking a Christmas lunch of roast potatoes and carrots, asparagus on toast and pineapple and melon for pudding, Bernard began to feel faint and took himself off to bed, immediately falling into a high fever and a fitful sleep. He had no idea of how much time passed but remembered waking up screaming every now and then. In his delirium, the walls and ceiling tried to crush him, and Titus, Emile and Zola's heads loomed over him, one moment monstrously gigantic, the next tiny as if he was zooming in on them through a camera lens.

Two days later, Bernard awoke to cheerful bird song and a concerned Ryan looking down at him.

'Still with us then,' said Ryan, who held a glass of water to Bernard's lips.

Bernard swallowed a few drops, enjoying the feeling of the liquid parching his thirst. As Ryan placed the glass on the bedside table, Bernard tried to sit up. But it felt as though his muscles had been replaced with jelly and he sank back onto the bed.

'Don't push yourself, Bernard. That's why you got so ill. The doctor says you need lots of rest.'

'But who's looking after Titus, Emile and Zola?'

'Don't worry about them!' said Ryan, rolling his eyes. 'They'll always be all right them lot. They never think about anyone but themselves.'

Bernard didn't have the energy to defend them. And to be honest, he didn't much feel up to it as he suddenly remembered the disastrous Christmas Eve and Christmas Day, memories that left an even nastier taste in his mouth than the one left by his fever. Anyway, he remembered them being here. On his bed looking after him, he was sure of it.

'I saw them...here in the room, on my bed,' he said.

'Now, now. Don't you be getting yourself all stressed about them monkeys. As I said, they'll be just fine.'

It all seemed like a dream to Bernard and, as he fell back to sleep, he resolved to ask Ryan when the monkeys could visit.

That evening, Bernard felt strong enough to sit up in bed and drink chicken soup Brenda had brought around.

'The house is very quiet,' said Bernard. 'Are they playing in their new treehouse?'

Ryan glared at the floorboards. 'The monkeys? No, Bernard. It's dark outside.'

'Are they inside playing with their marble run?'

Ryan shook his head, refusing to meet Bernard's eyes.

'I know they were looking after me...they must have fetched you.'

Ryan then looked straight at him. 'Oh, Bernard. They didn't fetch me. I popped round with your present on Christmas Day and found you with a high fever and them up here on your laptop to that Sebastian.'

'Perhaps they were asking him to contact a doctor or...'

'Bernard, Bernard, Bernard. I'm afraid to tell you, them monkeys have gone. Sebastian's chauffeur came to pick them up on Boxing Day.'

Once again Bernard recalled the unhappy events of Christmas Eve, how he'd come across them in the office being given a tour of Sebastian's mansion in Barbados and felt his heart breaking.

'They've flown to the Caribbean?' he asked, sadly.

'What? Oh no, looks like Sebastian asked to speak to you and they took the laptop up to your room. He took one look at you and decided the monkeys were a risk of catching whatever you had. They've gone back to London where Ding, Dang or Dong, whatever he calls them, will be safe from infection,' explained Ryan, impatiently.

Chapter 10

Bernard's strength steadily returned over the next few days, though his gloomy mood remained steadfast. As such, we find our hero sitting in his favourite threadbare armchair with a steaming mug of hot chocolate and a soggy-ended party horn dangling from his lips on New Year's Eve.

During his recovery, Bernard had much time to contemplate his short life and had come to two conclusions.

1. He was a destroyer of love.
2. He was free to travel again.

He blamed himself for losing the monkeys' love because it wasn't as if anyone hadn't tried to warn him about how naughty they were. Over the last two years, Ryan and Brenda had tried to get him to see he was too kind and indulgent and had not instilled enough discipline. It was something Bernard hadn't been keen to do because, well, he didn't much like being told off either. They'd suggested the monkeys may have respected him a little more if he'd been a bit tougher with them, though Bernard doubted that. They were monkeys, after all, and respected very little apart from bananas, acrobatics and asparagus on toast.

And anyway, perhaps it was his fault they treated him the way they did? Perhaps deep down they knew he deserved to be treated badly because of the unspeakable thing he had done? He remembered his parents saying that animals possess certain instincts humans have lost. That they can sense badness around them, in the shape of other creatures, or predicting events like earthquakes or deaths. The monkeys must have sensed that he was a bad person.

He knew he didn't deserve to be loved or happy after what he'd done. But looking after them had made him feel loved and happy for the first time since his parents had died.

What saddened Bernard the most, though, was realising the monkeys hadn't been worried about him while he was ill. He thought of all the times he'd nursed each of them back to health; Titus when he'd broken his left arm, Emile when he'd caught a bad chest infection and Zola when her tail had become trapped underneath a barn door and became infected. However, Bernard concluded that he was pleased to have looked after them, even though they may not have loved him the same way as he did them. The experience, he realised, had helped him deal with the whole horrid business of being orphanised.

Which led onto realisation number two. Could he really be free to travel and study anteaters now that the monkeys were living in London with Sebastian?

Some 23 million viewers had tuned into watch their performance on *Fame Me!* People were going crazy for them to appear on TV shows around the world. They had no need for Bernard and he wondered if they'd even remember him in a few months' time, let alone miss him. However, as much as

Bernard wanted to go off travelling again, there was a little nagging doubt in the pit of his stomach. Bernard had come to realise how vain, mean and selfish Sebastian was. But there was something else. He no longer trusted anything he said after all the broken promises of visiting at weekends.

What was it with adults, Bernard wondered, that they lied so much yet punished children for telling the smallest porkie pie? It was the same with Ms Snodgeweed, the headteacher at his school. She'd promised to look after him like a parent but instead spent her holidays looking after her supposedly sick relatives, always returning looking remarkably refreshed and sun tanned. Bernard had discovered the truth after checking her social media accounts and seeing all the photos of her and her friends sunbathing on tropical beaches and dancing on tables.

If Sebastian let him down so often, then what was to stop him letting down the monkeys? And if Bernard went travelling and anything happened between Sebastian and the monkeys, then they'd have nowhere to go and would probably end up in a zoo.

So, Bernard made a decision to stay in England for one year. If after the deadline the monkeys still preferred to live with Sebastian, then so be it. He would be free to travel.

Having made his first New Year's resolution, Bernard picked up the *Radio Times* and glanced down the list of programmes. He was looking forward to seeing one of his favourite films, *Harvey*, about a man followed around by a giant white rabbit, invisible only to him. It was due to start any minute but when he turned on the TV, he found the local news was still on.

It was a report about two tigers, who were cuddling up to one another in a small cage and Bernard was struck by how sad they looked. He turned up the volume to hear what the reporter, a glamorous lady with a short dark glossy bob, was saying.

'I'm at the Von Hesti Animal Park standing in front of the two tigers that allegedly mauled the reclusive billionaire, Baroness Bunny Von Hesti, to death last night in what police have described as a tragic and somewhat mysterious accident.'

Bernard sat up. The zoo was just a few miles away and he had many happy memories of visiting it with his parents, although he hadn't returned since their deaths. The screen switched to the presenter in the studio, a man wearing a bright blue suit and a fixed expression of concern.

'Can you tell us any more details?' he asked.

'Well, the police are refusing to tell us anything at this early stage but my sources say Bunny had gone to feed the tigers, who she'd hand-reared as babies and, for some mysterious reason, they turned on their mistress. It seems that her husband, Baron Von Hesti, had to go into the cage and retrieve his beloved wife's body.

'But the zoo workers here are mystified. They say the tigers loved Bunny and she worshipped them. It was, they say an attack totally out of character. Now what is interesting is that she'd recently had a hip replacement, she was, after all, 84 years old, and people are just wondering if she perhaps slipped and fell. And why did the tigers attack their beloved mistress? Well, maybe they were just having a bad day.

'However, what's really upsetting animal lovers across the world is that the hedge fund manager Baron Von Hesti,

Bunny's 11th husband, has declared he plans to shoot the tigers to avenge for his wife's death, as well as all the other animals in the zoo.'

The party horn in Bernard's mouth squeaked flatly and dropped onto his lap.

'He can't do that!' he shouted at the TV.

The screen went back to the presenter in the newsroom who asked exactly the same question poised on Bernard's lips.

'Why is he doing this? Surely, it isn't legal?'

'Well,' said the news reporter, 'he's obviously distraught by the death of his wife, who he only married two months ago at the zoo in this very cage with the tigers acting as witnesses.

'But, some sources close to the Baron, are saying that this isn't about revenge. It's about his hobbies of trophy hunting and canned hunting. For viewers who may not have heard the terms, trophy hunting is when animal reserves, mostly in Africa, allow rich people like Von Hesti to shoot big animals like lions and elephants in exchange for thousands of pounds which goes directly towards protecting the rest of the wildlife. Canned hunting is when lions are bred specially to be shot, a little like pheasants here... if you like. Both are controversial practices but ones which their defenders say help to fund the fight against poachers killing lions, rhinos and elephants for their bones, horns and tusks.

'Anyway, Von Hesti says now that his wife is dead, the zoo belongs to him and he can do exactly what he wants with the animals.'

The male presenter shook his head before asking: 'And how many animals are there?'

'There's 46 ranging from the tigers right down to a ginger

cat called Loki and a giant anteater who arrived just three months ago from Brazil. Hesti says he'll keep the zoo open this weekend and then it's curtains for all the animals.'

The camera panned onto an over-fluffed cat sleeping on a windowsill in the winter sunshine, then onto an anteater shielding itself from the cameras with its huge bristly tail, both oblivious to Baron Von Hesti's evil plan.

Bernard jumped out of his chair. 'He can't do that! You can't just shoot animals like that!' he shouted as the news-reader went onto a new report about rampaging squirrels in the nearby town of Folkestone, which on any other day Bernard would find fascinating.

But he was lost in his rage and his memories. Some of his happiest were of visiting the zoo with his parents. They used to spend whole days there, taking a picnic when the weather was mild. He'd loved the big cats, especially the tigers and sud-denly realised that the two who'd apparently mauled Baroness Von Hesti were probably the very same ones he'd spent hours admiring.

He loved the zoo most of all for inspiring his passion for anteaters. He still remembered the moment he spotted Cato, the giant anteater, his long nose grubbing around in the dirt for insects. Bernard must have been about four or five at the time. It had been love at first sight and he'd nagged his parents to take him there nearly every weekend. He tried to recall the last time he'd been there. It must have been at least three years ago when poor old Cato died of old age. It was the summer before his parents had died.

'What a terrible, terrible man!' he shouted.

And then, a seed of an idea took form and planted itself

firmly in his mind, rapidly growing until he had no other option than to act upon it.

Chapter 11

Bernard was looking forward to retracing a journey he'd made many times with his parents, the countryside changing from gentle valleys to sheer coastal drops as the train chugged along. However, he was definitely not looking forward to meeting the trigger happy Baron Von Hesti.

After posting a few lines on the hairless monkeys' official and unofficial websites about his plan, Bernard had spent the rest of the evening searching for information about the Baron. He'd felt a flicker of recognition as he trawled through all the internet images of the vile man, mostly taken at parties, looking drunk and boss-eyed.

There was definitely something familiar about him. Bernard couldn't quite put his finger on it but he'd seen him somewhere before, either on TV or in a newspaper. He wasn't sure if it was the jutting jaw, or the way his mouth turned down at the corners as if he was disappointed with life, despite being one of the richest men in the world.

As he researched the Baron, one thing grew clear: the man enjoyed posting pictures of himself posing with his latest hunting trophy, a lifeless and bloodied rhino, elephant or lion, hugging his semi-automatic gun to him like a much-cherished child. Bernard discovered he was one of a small number of rich, mostly, male, humans who paid thousands of pounds to legally shoot animals in a wildlife park in the name of conservation. The money they paid apparently employed more wardens to protect those rhinos and elephants lucky enough not to be shot and butchered by poachers. Like the glamorous TV reporter had said, it was a controversial practice and one that his parents had campaigned against before they died.

The practice also left Bernard feeling very uneasy, though he had more immediate concerns to worry about: namely how Von Hesti would react to his plan.

Because it really wasn't very much of a plan at all.

He was going to ask him nicely if he'd let the animals live and offer to find them homes.

On a Sunday.

At 9am in the morning.

And as he sat on the train admiring the sea's jade stripes, he prayed that a few people reading the monkeys' fan sites may feel the same way and come to support him. He'd even phoned Sebastian to ask if he could lend his high-profile support and bring Emile, Zola and Titus along. But Sebastian had refused, saying they were far too busy to get involved.

However, as Bernard got off the train and turned the corner into the zoo entrance, he realised he needn't have worried.

A wall of hundreds of protestors was waiting for him, waving an assortment of banners and posters, reading: *Hands off Bunny's animals! No hunting in Bunny's name! Shame on you, Von Nasti!*

Bernard was amazed to see many of the protesters had even followed his suggestion to form human barricades around each of the enclosures. As Bernard joined the protesters outside the tigers' enclosures, shouting: 'We will, we will not be moved!' he saw a man in a pair of blue and red striped pyjamas racing across the front lawn of the Von Hesti mansion, his half-on dressing gown flapping behind him like a broken wing.

Bernard recognised the man as Von Hesti straight away from the internet images.

'You're trespassing on private property,' Von Hesti bellowed as he came closer, squinting at the lines of protestors before him.

'It's a public zoo,' shouted Bernard through the loudspeaker his parents had once regularly used to call him in for tea.

'Not anymore!' replied Von Hesti as he rummaged around in his dressing gown pocket, trying and failing to locate something. 'I've decided it's closed from now. Shut. Fechado. There will be no animals to see! Although you'd be very welcome to see them adorning my walls and floors once they're skinned,' he laughed.

There was a collective gasp from the protestors who surged forwards, shouting out names you can't repeat in a children's book.

'You'll have to shoot us first!' Bernard said into his loudspeaker as four burly bodyguards, also still in their stripy pyjamas, came running from the house.

Von Hesti inched forwards until he came nose to nose with a placard bearing a photo of a furry black and white creature. It was being held by a little girl, standing with a group of children. He stabbed at the creature's face with a fat stumpy finger, his features twisting into a mask of pure hatred.

'These monsters killed my beloved Bunny!' he shouted, leaving a splattering of dribble over the picture.

'It's a baby lemur,' said the little girl holding the placard. 'He didn't kill your wife.'

Von Hesti spun round, trying to find the owner of the voice.

'Oh, it's only a matter of time before they'd all be at it. Lemurs and all their despicable furry friends. Reverting to the wild, savaging the hand that feeds them. And I'm not going to wait to be their next feast, thank you very much.'

'What? Even Bunny's cat?' said a boy, standing next to the little girl.

'Who said that?' growled Von Hesti, peering down at a group of giggling children. 'Yes, even the cat! Why do you think they stare at you so? They're wondering how to go about eating you and what you'll taste like!

'It's all very well, you village children and your peasant parents, thinking that animals are all nicey-nicey fluffy and cuddly. Well, let me tell you, this isn't *Build a Bear*. These beasts have real teeth, claws, tusks and horns that will rip you apart at the drop of a hat,' he snarled, saliva flying over the protestors who quickly shielded themselves with their placards.

'Now listen to me and you all listen carefully,' he added, his voice becoming deeper and more menacing. 'My beloved Bunny left everything to me. It's got nothing to do with you. Now GET OFF MY LAND!'

Bernard gulped and stepped forward.

'Excuse me, Mr Von Hesti. I'll pay you for the animals.'

'It's Baron Von Hesti...wherever you are,' he said peering at a placard of another lemur, 'glasses! I need my glasses!'

Each of the bodyguards pulled out a shiny gold glasses case, offering them to the Baron. He snatched one of the cases and, as he fiddled around trying to open it, Bernard's eye was caught by a thin young woman with bright red hair running towards them from the mansion. She was dressed in a pink dressing gown and matching slippers which were looking decidedly mud-coloured by the time she reached Von Hesti.

'Darling, what's happening? The shoot's tomorrow. Everyone is arriving today to choose. You need to get rid of these idiots,' she said, pulling at his sleeve before trying to bat the protestors away like flies.

'Shoo! Go away! The zoo is closed. Go and do whatever peasanty things you do on a Sunday...go on, away with you! Bring the turnip harvest in or something useful,' she added, now inching away from the protesters as if they were diseased.

'It will be fine,' Von Hesti muttered, 'and how many times do I have to tell you, don't call me darling,' he snarl-whispered.

Von Hesti finally managed to open the case and put on his glasses.

'Now, who mentioned money?'

Bernard's hand shot up and the Baron gestured to him to come closer using a long claw-like middle finger. Bernard walked towards the Baron, his stomach somersaulting, a little like a hairless monkey's performance but this one on a boat at sea. In a storm. With ten metre waves. And loads of sharks circling. He didn't do confrontation. He couldn't even confront the monkeys about their bad behaviour. And now...

He stopped in front of the sneering Baron who pushed his face into Bernard's. He was just about to back away, when a memory stirred. His eyes narrowed as he remembered being in the Amazon, just moments before he found the monkeys. He'd been tracking a giant anteater when he'd heard a snap of a twig and glanced up to see a man through the foliage about to take aim with a huge rifle. The man had heard Bernard and glanced round. But Bernard had already ducked out of sight behind the giant Kaypok tree. Bernard's brilliant blue eyes grew into oceans as he looked into the Baron's own slithers of black ditch water.

The man before him was the same man who'd killed the monkeys' mother, he was sure of it. He'd only snatched a glimpse of the murderer through the thick leaves and twisted vines but he'd recognise those cold shark eyes anywhere. But there was something else about him. He'd seen him even before that, he was sure of it, as a distant memory tugged at him before slipping away.

'What a scruffy lot of beggars you are!' he said looking down at Bernard who hadn't time to brush his thick dark sticky up hair and was wearing his dad's old hat and jacket, a pair of muddy jeans and a dog-eared pair of boots.

But Bernard wasn't listening. He was being consumed by a sudden silent rage boiling up inside him. He stepped forward and squared up to Von Hesti. Though at least two feet shorter and much wirier than the overweight Baron, his anger made him feel like a super hero.

'You don't scare me, peasant! I could squash you like an ant,' said Von Hesti, squishing gravel with his slipper, his upper lip curling as if he would gobble up Bernard like one of the lions he was so fond of shooting.

'Well, I am not ant. I am here to demand on behalf of all these people that you leave the animals alone.'

'Demand? Who are you to demand anything from me, Baron Von Hesti, the third richest person in the universe?'

'My name is Bernard Bamuel and I know what you did.'

Von Hesti's jaw dropped as Bernard drew closer.

'Bamuel, you say?' he said taking a step back.

Bernard nodded, realising he must have read about him and seen the monkeys performing on *Fame Me!* They were even more famous than the Queen, according to Brenda who'd read a recent poll in one of the celebrity magazines.

'Four words, Baron Von Hesti,' whispered Bernard.

'That's ...actually...five already,' stuttered the Baron whose eyes grew so wide that Bernard hoped they may pop out onto the ground and be snaffled up by the murder of crows watching events unfold from a nearby oak tree.

Indeed, he was so alarmed by the effect he was having on the baron that the four words he was meant to say – Amazon, hairless monkeys' mother - got bored and floated away.

Instead, out came one simple, far, far more powerful one.

'Murderer!'

The word hit Von Hesti like a bullet and he stumbled backwards into his bodyguards, the colour draining from his face as if he'd seen the ghosts of all the animals he'd ever shot trailing past one by one.

'The shoot is off,' he whimpered. 'Give him what he wants.'

Chapter 12

I, Baron Von Hesti, give the Von Hesti Animal Park and all its animals to Bernard Bamuel of Fluffingdale Farm. In return, I ask that you (Bernard Bamuel) must never accuse me of being a murderer ever again, or the deal is off.

'With pleasure,' said Bernard pulling out another page and reading:

Below is a list of the animals now belonging to you:

1. Two (murderous) tigers

2. Four giraffes

3. Two zebras

4. Four gorillas

5. Six mandrills

6. Five warthogs

7. Twenty-one lemurs (including two rare dancing lemurs)

8. One domestic cat

9. One giant anteater.

'My very own giant anteater! Yipeeeeeee,' celebrated Bernard, doing a solo congo around the house and imagining all the adventures they'd share.

Ten minutes later, he found himself dancing into the office and coming to a sudden halt in front of the mantelpiece. Dozens of photo frames covered in thick dust and fine cobwebs stood with their backs to him. He'd turned the happy photos of his parents to face the wall just after their funerals. He couldn't bear to see them staring at him, knowing what they knew about him.

He put out his hand to turn the largest photo of them around. It was his favourite and as such, was imprinted on his mind forever. He was sitting in the garden under the cherry tree in full blossom with his mum and dad. He must have been about four or five at the time. They were all laughing because his dad had set the timer and then tripped over on his way back and only half of him was visible in the photo.

They may not be able to forgive me but, surely, they'd be proud of me? thought Bernard as his hand hovered over the dusty frame. Standing up to bullies like Von Hesti and saving the zoo animals was exactly the kind of campaign his parents would have got involved in, he realised.

But as Bernard fingers touched the frame, he felt a little electric shock and snatched his hand away. I am nothing compared to them, he told himself. And never will be.

He turned away from the mantelpiece.

'Once I sign this letter, I'm going to own a zoo,' said Bernard out loud, realising how mad that sounded.

And then a memory hit him so violently that Bernard flinched. He remembered overhearing his parents arguing about taking him to the zoo so often.

His mother had complained that keeping animals locked up in cages or enclosures to be gawped at was cruel and Bernard could learn more about them by watching wildlife documentaries. His father agreed the concept of zoos was bad, unless they helped conservation. But, he'd added, wasn't it cruel to deny their son the chance to see the wonderful animals in real life, just a few miles away?

Surely they'd be happy to see him saving the animals? he thought to himself. It wasn't as if he was going to add more animals. He didn't really have a plan except to save the animals and keep it going until, well, until the animals died and then? Well, then who knew what would happen?

He slumped into his armchair and re-read the letter several times, trying to let the words sink in. And, as he did so, another far more troublesome worry than the memory of his parents arguing about the rights and wrongs of zoos popped in his head. He couldn't quite put his finger on it but something just didn't sound right.

Every time he re-read the letter, he paused over the last sentence. *Please sign and return at your leisure.*

It puzzled him that Von Hesti had handed the zoo over so easily. Was a man famed for shooting defenceless animals really that frightened of what the world thought of him for killing the monkeys' mother? Bernard knew that Titus, Emile and Zola were huge stars now. But he'd never imagined the power they wielded. Perhaps, he feared if word got out he'd killed the mother of the most popular acrobats in the world, he'd be shunned forever by his rich friends?

However, from what Bernard had learnt of Von Hesti, his sudden concern for what people think of him was completely out of character. He was so rich he didn't care what anyone thought of him. He could behave how he liked because there were no consequences. This was the man, after all, who boasted on social media that his New Year resolution was to kill more lions, rhinos and elephants than any other person in the world.

But, perhaps, Bernard was being unfair to judge him so harshly? Perhaps he'd had change of heart after all, (though he doubted Von Hesti possessed such a thing).

Anyway, the animals were his priority for now. There was no point worrying about Von Hesti's motives. What was important was that Bernard and the protestors had won. They had saved the animals.

Bernard signed the agreement.

Chapter 13

Over the next few weeks Bernard and the zookeepers set about transforming the zoo to its former glory. All the protestors had pledged their weekends and holidays to help do up the animal enclosures in time for a summer opening and Bernard threw himself into contacting all the carpenters and builders, who on hearing about his bravery in standing up to Von Hesti, offered their services free of charge.

For the first time since the monkeys had deserted him, Bernard began to feel that there could be life beyond Zola, Titus and Emile. He now had a zoo full of orphanised creatures to look after, not to mention his two new companions, Bunny's incredibly fluffy ginger cat, Loki and, of course, Armando, the anteater.

Like the tigers, Mr Stripy and Marley, who had allegedly killed Bunny, Loki and Armando had looked upon her as their surrogate mother and were grieving for her in their own ways. Loki had been with Bunny since a kitten, while Armando had come from a zoo in Venezuela as a two-year-old straight after weaning. While Loki refused to move from his favourite window since his mistress had died, Armando refused to emerge from the cover of his thick bushy tail and both spurred all offers of food and comfort.

Bernard visited them every day, leaving behind fresh sardines, chicken and other treats for Loki, and worm mush and over-ripe pears for Armando. But every time he returned, neither had touched the food. They were behaving in the same way as Marley and Mr Stripy, who were also refusing to eat as they pined away for Bunny.

On the fifth day, before he left for home, Bernard checked on Loki and was shocked to see how much weight he'd lost. There was nothing left of him apart from a flatish and rather dull wodge of tangled ginger fur, reminding Bernard of his poor teddies after the monkeys had de-stuffed them. Too weak to bite and scratch, he allowed Bernard to pick him up, and take him home. He took him upstairs to his bedroom and lay him down on his duvet.

After a couple of days of accepting a few cat biscuits and a little water, Loki held out a paw to Bernard and allowed him to hold and stroke it. The next day, he began to eat the sardines Bernard mashed up specially for him and after a couple of weeks his appetite for food and life began to return. He allowed Bernard to brush his unruly fur, even on his tummy, without biting and scratching, and began to follow him everywhere, even accompanying him on the train to the zoo, returning to Fluffingdale in the evenings where he'd curl up on Bernard's lap in front of the TV.

Armando proved harder to cheer up. The zookeepers told Bernard there was nothing they could do. You couldn't force an animal, especially an anteater like Armando to eat. He had a reputation for stubbornness, they told Bernard, refusing to be fed and watered by anyone other than Bunny herself.

On the seventh day, Bernard went and sat with Armando,

whose breathing was becoming shallower and shallower. He stayed with him all day, stroking his straw-like hair, singing nursery rhymes and the poems that his mum used to read to him over and over again, including the only one he knew about an anteater:

'A genuine anteater,' the pet shop told me dad.
Turned out it was an aunt eater
And now my uncle's mad!

He also regaled Armando with some of his favourite anteater jokes like:

What topping does an anteater have on his pizza? Antchovies!

Why don't anteaters get ill? Because they're full of anty-bodies!

When the anteater lost the race to the ant what did he say? If you can't beat them, eat them.

However, no amount of groan-worthy jokes got the slightest squeak out of Armando. Some would say with jokes that bad, reader, was it any wonder Armando remained under his tail of despair? But Bernard was not to be dissuaded.

'Perhaps I should translate them into Portuguese and then he'd get them?' he wondered out loud one day in front of Brenda, who was to take over the running of the zoo gift shop.

'Or perhaps, if you don't mind me saying, Bernard, that you're not thinking this through properly. Perhaps, he does understand the jokes but the real crux of the matter is anteaters don't possess a sense of humour,' she said.

It was a sentence that struck Bernard speechless for a few moments because it was obvious that if you looked like an anteater then, of course, you had to have a sense of humour.

Bernard wasn't going to stop trying to cheer up Armando because, if he did, then we'd never get to the end of the story. Gradually, Armando allowed Bernard to lift up his tail of doom and stroke his head without his claws shooting out threateningly.

But the event that changed everything happened one fine spring day when Loki wandered into the pen looking for Bernard. Armando happened to lift his head at the same time as Loki's entrance and his long nose accidently dipped into Loki's fur and the rest is history. It was love at first sight, or at the very least, at first touch. The two became inseparable and Armando began the daily commute to and from the zoo with Bernard and Loki, often carrying the latter on his back in the evening.

In terms of the tigers, Bernard could hardly use the same tactics to win them around. And anyway, even if Bernard could have taken them home with him, he wasn't sure he wanted to. Would you want to comfort two man-eating tigers?

But he had to do something. The tigers were wasting away. Their glossy stripes were discoloured and dulled by dirt and dust. And their beautiful amber eyes, when they bothered to open them, wept constantly. Bernard knew that the public would be happy to see the tigers in their current state because, although it was hard to know why, he understood from all the TV dramas that people have a greedy troll's appetite for all things involving death and cruelty to other people and to animals.

As for Bernard, he had mixed feelings about the tigers. They had killed their mistress, who had brought them up as babies. They had essentially orphanised themselves; a fact that Bernard found very disagreeable, mainly because he was guilty of doing the same. What right did he, or they have to be depressed when they had killed their loving mothers?

Anyway, could tigers really feel sadness and regret? Surely, they were cold-hearted killers like the Baron?

Whatever, the cause of their depression, Bernard decided to take action. Although he wouldn't be able to smother them with affection like he did with Loki and Armando, he could smother them with attention. So, two weeks before the zoo opened, he spent four hours a day outside their cage talking to them gently, whispering that they mustn't blame themselves for Bunny's death. It wasn't their fault. It was the tiger in them. They couldn't help themselves. And that Bunny loved them very much and would never have blamed them. That she would have hated to see them looking so sad.

And slowly but surely, the tigers' tempers improved and they began to get their appetites and energy back. They started to leave their cage and explore their upgraded mini-jungle, though they lumbered around like they couldn't quite be bothered, only taking a few steps before lying back down again with their backs to the world.

Two days before the zoo was due to open Bernard inspected all the animals to make sure they were happy to be showed to the public. He ended up at the tiger cage, wondering whether they were really ready to be gawped at and gossiped about by the visitors. Mr Stripy was half-headedly sharpening his nails on a tree while Marley dozed. Both their coats were shining again and their eyes had stopped watering.

But Bernard realised as he watched them, they had lost the

very tigerness that had caused their downfall. They may as well have been two stuffed cuddly toys.

'You will have to do,' said Bernard as he turned to watch the builders place the brand new sign onto the gates spelling out Fluffingdale Zoo.

Chapter 14

'I thought they could be guests of honour and cut the ribbon,' Bernard suggested over the phone. 'And... you, of course, Sebastian,' he'd forced himself to add.

'No can do, Bernie. We're on our sell out European tour and will be travelling to Dublin that night.'

'Couldn't you just pop in on the way?'

'I know the monkeys are talented, Bernie, but I think sky-diving from a private jet may be asking a little too much,' Sebastian replied, sarcastically. 'Anyway, my PR lady says Ding, Do... I mean the monkeys...,' he quickly corrected himself, 'shouldn't be associated with the zoo. It may damage their image.'

'What...?'

'They're at the peak of their fame. Zoos don't fit in with their brand,' interrupted Sebastian. 'Anyway, gotta go.'

Bernard heard the familiar noise of the line going dead as Sebastian ended the call. It was true the monkeys fame had skyrocketed. After appearing on *Fame Me!* they'd been signed up for a European tour which sold out in ten seconds. But surely being seen to save other animals would be great for their so-called 'brand' whatever that meant?

Bernard didn't approve of the monkeys' lifestyles and the

way they'd so happily embraced Sebastian and fame, though he couldn't live without the money Sebastian transferred into his account every month. It was far more than he'd ever imagined and far more than he could ever spend. In the meantime, he decided, it was best to be a richish hypocrite than be poor.

Although the zoo was very soon paying for itself, the money the monkeys earned would be handy to pay for vets' bills and any extras and, of course, keep the house running. However, deep down, Bernard secretly wished that the monkeys would one day grow bored of being adored by millions and come home. Now he had Loki and Armando at his side and the zoo to keep him occupied, Bernard had forgiven the monkeys for deserting him at Christmas. He tried calling them occasionally, but they were always perfecting their performance, in make-up, or having their costumes fitted, Sebastian told him.

'Far too busy to be disturbed, Bernie,' was Sebastian's stock reply. Or a dismissive, 'I'll tell them you called.'

So, the opening of the zoo went ahead without their special guest appearances and the summer disappeared as fast a politician's promise and, before Bernard knew it, another Christmas was upon him.

He already knew the monkeys wouldn't come home; Sebastian had told him that the monkeys wanted to remain in London as they were busy preparing for a very special show in front of the Queen, the Royal Variety Performance on Christmas Day. They were then jetting off to Sebastian's Barbadian mansion with the creepy Virgil Boghero. Bernard tried hard not to mind too much.

He'd invited Ryan and Bob over to watch the performance, and then Brenda had invited herself over when she discovered Ryan was coming. They would settle down in front of the fire with some toasted crumpets and watch it together.

He'd be far happier watching the monkeys on the TV in the comfort of his own home beside Loki and Armando, away from the hustle and bustle of London.

And well, he couldn't go even if he wanted to because he'd given all the zoo keepers a week off over the festive period and therefore had to feed all the animals.

And, well, anyway, he hadn't actually been invited.

Chapter 15

During the early hours of Christmas Eve, Bernard gave up trying to sleep as waves of angry and resentful thoughts about Sebastian crashed over him. The question as to why he hadn't been invited to the monkeys' most prestigious performance kept replaying over and over again. He'd love to see them perform in a posh London theatre and couldn't understand why Sebastian hadn't thought to invite him.

It was me who saved them, me who trained them, me who brought them up! You'd think the least he could do was invite me along, even if I can't go.

Then, at exactly 6.10am, Bernard sat bolt upright as a cold stark realisation hit him over the head several dozen times.

'He's stolen them!' he shouted into the early morning quiet, waking Loki and Armando, who both sprang up as one beast from the bottom of the bed. 'Shhh...it's okay. Go back to sleep,' Bernard whispered, reaching out into the dark to pat them as they settled back down.

Bernard lay back on the bed, recalling all the times in the early days when he'd tried to get Sebastian to bring the monkeys down at weekends and all his excuses about early nights being essential to their training. Yet he'd seen the evidence in the newspapers and from Brenda; the monkeys were out every night with Sebastian and that Virgil Boghero. And to top it all, he kept on calling him Bernie even though he'd corrected him several billion times.

'No-one else but my parents are allowed to call me Bernie,' he whispered.

Just as he was pondering on how he could win back the monkeys' affections from Sebastian, a frenzied banging erupted at the front door.

'Who, what and why?' said Bernard as he slipped out of bed and crept to the window.

He pulled open the curtains, peering into the grey fuzz of dawn, wondering if it was Ryan or Brenda at the door. However, there were no signs of tyre tracks in the fine sprinkling of snow lying on the driveway. It lay undisturbed, except for a single pair of human footsteps leading to the front door. Bernard stood on his tiptoes, craning his neck. He could just make out a shadowy outline standing outside the porch, looking up at the house and suddenly Bernard's imagination conjured up all sorts of axe-wielding visitors to Fluffingdale Farm.

He shrunk away from the window and examined the size of the footsteps in the snow. They were smaller than his, he was sure of it, and therefore, in all probability, posed no physical threat, unless, of course, it was a troll with very small feet. The mystery visitor banged on the door again and Bernard ran down the hallway, followed closely behind by the ever-inquisitive Armando carrying a sleepy Loki on his back.

'Just coming,' said Bernard, his breath leaving behind little puffs of cloud like a steam engine as he raced down the stairs.

Bernard flicked on the light switch, blinking back the glare. He quickly unlocked the door and gingerly opened it to see a slight figure, about the same size as him, dressed in an oversized parka, wellington boots and a bobble hat.

Bernard peered into the stranger's face trying to place it, thinking it must be someone from the village or a passing motorist whose car had broken down on the road nearby, although the driver definitely looked younger than 17. Then it spoke.

'It's cold out here if you haven't noticed. Aren't you going to invite me in?' the female voice said.

Before he had a chance to reply, she'd barged through the door, coming to a sudden stop as she clocked Armando.

'Woah! Is that an anteater... wearing a ginger fur coat?' she said, scuttling back towards the door.

'Well, I suppose it is,' said Bernard, who was now seeing the Armando and Loki combination through new eyes. 'But the fur coat is a cat and it looks like he's gone back to sleep.'

'My uncle said you were a bit weird,' she said, tentatively patting Armando's head as his long nose carried out a frenzied sniffing inspection of her knees.

Bernard weighed up whether to ignore the comment. He supposed that many people in the village thought him odd. But still.

'It's a bit too early in the morning to be insulted,' Bernard said.

'Oh, I didn't mean to be rude,' she replied. 'I've come about Emile, Titus and Zola.'

Bernard rolled his eyes to the ceiling. Of course, the strange visitor was a fan! None had called round since the monkeys had moved to London. But, perhaps, this one was chancing her luck, thinking they'd be home for Christmas, Bernard wondered.

'I do admire your dedication. But you've a wasted journey. They're not coming home for Christmas. They live in London now. You need to get in touch with Sebastian Trophy-Assetclass's agent...I have her name somewhere...if you want to email me?' said Bernard, wheeling out his standard reply for the monkeys' intrepid fans.

'No, no, no! I know where they are. With my uncle, unfortunately,' said the stranger.

'What? Sebastian?'

The girl nodded.

'You're his...,' paused Bernard trying to work out the connection, 'niece?'

'Unluckily, yes,' she said, pulling off her bobble hat, freeing a head full of bouncy light brown curls.

As he watched them tumble over her shoulders, a tickle of a memory teased him, only to disappear for a moment before charging back in full colour and top of the volume stereo.

'You were at his house in Barbados, cleaning his cinema? I thought you were the maid!'

'I may as well be the way he treats me.'

'Why do you live with him then?'

'It's a long story but I don't have much choice.' She held her hand out. 'I'm Larold.'

'L-A-R-O-L-D?' repeated Bernard slowly, shaking her hand at the same speed.

'Sadly, yes. My parents weren't sure if I was going to be a boy or a girl so they decided to combine their two favourite names...Harold with Lara.'

Bernard winced.

'Tell me about it.'

'But he never mentioned he had a niece living with him?'

'No surprise there. My uncle keeps lots of secrets. And I'm one of them. Talking of which you need to watch this,' she said, getting her phone out of her pocket. 'It's Titus, Emile and Zola. They're in great danger.'

'What do you mean? What's happened?' asked Bernard, panicking.

'Don't worry. They're fine for now. Look. I've come quite a long way. In the snow. Any chance of a cup of tea?'

Bernard led her into kitchen, put the kettle on and lit the fire he'd set the night before.

'I knew my uncle must be up to something more than just making money out of your monkeys,' said Larold, pulling up one of the kitchen chairs. 'You see, he hates animals and children which is why he treats me the way he does,' she explained as Bernard made a pot of tea.

'But he said he loved them like they were his own!' said Bernard, his face reddening. 'They never wanted to speak to me when he took them away. I thought they preferred him to me.'

'He's such a liar. He love-bombed them at first -'

'Love bombed?' interrupted Bernard.

'Spoiled them rotten for the first few months, showering them with presents, to get them to like him, telling them they were amazing and how much he loved them and how it was such a shame that you didn't want to look after them anymore, and then when he'd won them over, he turfed them into the garage with me.'

'The garage?' said Bernard, imagining the poor monkeys sleeping on a cold hard concrete floor, huddled together for warmth.

'Sleeping in the garage is a walk in the park compared to what he's got planned for them,' explained Larold. 'Sebastian had two visitors last night. I recorded them talking...I was awake all night. I didn't know what to do, so I sneaked out and got the first train from London.'

'What plans?' asked Bernard, feeling like his whole world was one big snow globe once again being shaken up by Sebastian.

All sorts of horrible thoughts ran through his head as he imagined Sebastian forcing them to leap through hoops of fire while being pursued by starving lions, or being flung from high buildings onto a trampoline, or worst still, a cheap mattress.

'We don't have much time. Just watch this and I'll explain,' she said as she pressed play.

Bernard sat down next to Larold and did as she asked. The video showed a palatial sitting room, the gold walls decorated with dozens of pictures of Sebastian on his own, or posing with different celebrities including the hideous Virgil Boghero.

'I had to put the phone on the tea tray,' explained Larold as the lens jolted, revealing a very boring white ceiling. Three faces then loomed into view on screen as she poured and handed out cups of tea.

'Eek!' said Bernard as he recognised the first, the smokey bacon orange face of Virgil Boghero. The second belonged to Sebastian and the third, a middle-aged Chinese lady. Her bright red lipstick had bled into the little lines around her lips making it look as though her mouth was stitched on.

'Who's she?' asked Bernard.

'Dr Karen Wu. A grinder of tiger bones, rhino horn, elephant tusks and...hairless monkeys to make quack medicines for her clients in the Far East.'

Bernard felt a hard blow to his tummy. It was as if someone with a huge lump of wood, had taken a run up to him from a great distance and then whacked him in the stomach. He opened his mouth to speak but only a funny gasping squeak came out.

'I'm afraid so,' said Larold, patting him on the back and pausing the film. 'Maybe I shouldn't show you the rest.'

'No, no. I want to see,' said Bernard, pleased to have found his voice again.

Larold nodded and pressed play.

'You can go now. Go on...away child,' Sebastian said, followed by a pshtting noise as if he was shooing away a cat. The video showed Larold taking the tray and her phone into the kitchen and then stopped.

'That Dr Wu really gave me the creeps so I sneaked back and listened behind the door to see what they were up to. And I'm glad I did,' she said pressing the play button and turning up the volume.

'I trust you had a good flight?' asked Sebastian.

'Yes, very good. Very quick. No small talk Mr Trophy Asse-Cass.'

'Assetclass,' corrected Sebastian.

'That's what I say,' replied the doctor. 'Let's get down to business. My flight leave for Shanghai in two hour.'

'Of course, of course. Now how long will it take?' asked Virgil.

An image of the grey creature and the bald man on the sun lounger in Barbados flashed up in Bernard's mind. He looked at Larold, his eyes widening as he finally made the connection. It was no furry grey animal he'd seen on his sunlounger. It was Boghero's wig.

'Virgil's bald?'

Larold paused the recording. 'As a baby's bottom.'

'So it's Boghero who wants the monkeys' bones to cure his baldness?'

'And Sebastian.'

'What? But that doesn't make any sense. He's always going on about how luscious his hair is in all those awful shampoo adverts?'

'Keep up, Bernard. He's got a room full of wigs,' she said.

Bernard's mouth was now hanging open. He was unsure what was more shocking; the famous hair adverts being a complete con, or what Sebastian and Virgil wanted to do with his beloved monkeys.

'Now listen,' she said, pressing play again.

It was Dr Wu's voice this time. 'As soon as monkey dead, I need to slice 'n' dice. Chippety-choppety-chop. Just like that. Into little cubes, Lego size. Then boil up bones to get rid of meat and skin and then dry in hot sun or oven. Eight hours tops or sometimes...'

'No, no, no...' interrupted Sebastian. 'I think Mr Boghero meant how long will it take for our hair to grow back?'

'Ah! Very quick. Hairless monkey excellent for baldies like

you. Rub magic lotion on twice day and in two months your hair thick like forest,' said the doctor.

'Well, that's excellent, Dr Wu,' said Sebastian, 'though I'm not sure Mr Boghero or I will be up for actually...you know...the..kkkkk..how do you call it...er....'

'You want me kill monkey?' asked Dr Wu.

'Now that's an idea, isn't it, Virgil?'

'Mmmm,' replied Virgil as if he had never thought of it before.

'It bring me big happiness to kill monkey. All three. Monkey steal handbag and camera on holiday in Gibraltar and pull wing mirror off hire car last year, then I crash car into tourist bus and break leg 'cos I can't see nothing without wing mirror. I HATE monkey.'

'Well, Dr Wu, that would be excellent,' said Sebastian. 'If we pay extra you could come to our house in Barbados on Boxing Day?'

'No, no, no! I no want extra. I kill monkey for pleasure. The price remain £1 million as agreed.'

Bernard held his head in hands, mostly trying to stop the tears from falling. He didn't want to cry in front of a stranger. Larold paused the recording as Sebastian showed Dr Wu out.

'There's more. Are you sure you want to listen to it?' she asked.

Bernard wiped his eyes with the back of his hand and nodded. Larold pressed play again and they listened to the sound of two teacups being clinked together.

'To a thick head of hair once more!' said Virgil's rasping voice.

'To the hairless monkeys,' said Sebastian, laughing.

'What about that Bamuel boy. The poor idiot is awfully fond of the creatures. What are we going to tell him?' asked Virgil.

'Ahh, leave Bernie to me. What can he do stuck in England, anyway? We'll be in Barbados. No-one will ever know the truth,' said Sebastian, before putting on a high-pitched sickly voice.

'Bernie, I'm so, sooooo sorry. Those monkeys were soooo naughty, soooo curious. They must have got up in the night and oh dear...boo, hoo, I found them floating face down in the swimming pool.'

'Boo, hoo. They were just like my babies,' added Virgil, now both of them laughing hysterically.

Now it was Bernard's turn to press pause.

'I've heard enough,' he said.

Chapter 16

That afternoon, Bernard travelled to Sebastian's London house on the pretext of dropping off surprise Christmas presents to Emile, Zola and Titus. During the train journey, he fantasised about barging into the house and punching Sebastian on the nose before snatching Emile, Zola and Titus and taking them home.

He was furious that Sebastian would exploit the monkeys so ruthlessly; making a fortune out of their talent and then kill them for a quack baldness cure.

But as Bernard got closer to London his anger began to give way to fear. What if Sebastian wouldn't allow him to see the monkeys? What if they'd gone out? What if the monkeys didn't want to come with him, or didn't understand the danger they were in?

Worse still, what if they didn't rescue them in time and the unspeakable happened? Bernard took a deep breath to calm his racing heart as the taxi pulled into Sebastian's street, Clifton Crescent. He jumped out of the cab just as a group of carol singers came round the corner. They were glancing up and down the road and Bernard overheard them discussing whether they'd be welcome at the huge imposing mansions.

'That's if anyone actually lives in them. Bet most of the

owners live abroad,' said a lady wearing a floppy pink bobble hat, rubbing her hands together to keep warm.

Bernard suddenly had a brainwave and walked over to the group.

'I hope you don't think I'm being nosey but I overheard what you said. I'm just about to visit my good friend Sebastian Trophy-Assetclass who, as you may know, loves singers.'

'What? *The* Sebastian Trophy-Assetclass from *Fame Me!*?' asked a little girl of no more than seven or eight.

'Yes, the very same,' said Bernard, bending down slightly and smiling.

'He was only telling me yesterday how Christmas isn't the same without any carol singers and here you are!'

'Oh, Mummy, please can we go and see the nice man off the telly?' the girl asked the bobble-hatted lady, who glanced around at the rest of the group before shrugging.

'We were just wondering if it's worth it as most of his type won't even answer their doors,' she said.

'I can guarantee we'll open the door for you. Number 34. Just give us a few minutes.'

Bernard crossed the road and ambled along the street casually as if he knew where he was going. Larold had told him he'd be unable to miss the house, a huge five storey mansion with a lurid gold front door bearing the number 34 in shiny black letters and sure enough, Bernard soon came across it. He rang the doorbell and then knocked just in case Larold hadn't heard. Glancing back down the street, he smiled as he saw the group of carol singers crossing the road further down. He waved, then turned back to see Larold standing at the open door, dressed in a black and white maid's uniform.

'Who shall I say is calling?' she said loudly while Bernard mouthed 'I have a plan' and gestured to the approaching carol singers.

Sebastian's voice boomed in the background: 'If it's carol singers, tell them I need to rest my ears.'

Bernard went to step into the hallway but felt himself being propelled back onto the doorstep as Sebastian suddenly appeared and pushed Larold out of the way.

'Oh, what are you doing here?' he asked as if Bernard was something nasty he'd stepped in. 'I thought I told you it'd be too unsettling to see them and anyway, we've got rehearsals.'

'Er...Happy Christmas!' Bernard exclaimed in a mock-cheery voice, quickly placing his foot in the door just as Sebastian tried to close it. 'I was in London anyway, and I thought I'd give the monkeys a few extra gifts for the holiday,' he said, pushing the door with his shoulder and stepping into the hallway.

'Their holiday?' asked Sebastian, his botoxed brow trying hard to furrow as he tried to usher Bernard out.

'Yes, Barbados, remember?' said Bernard, pushing the door open a fraction.

'Oh, yes, of course. Barbados. How could I forget...but they have everything they need. We're all packed and ready, thank you,' said Sebastian, shoving the door against Bernard.

Bernard pushed back and glanced nervously behind, mentally berating the carol singers to hurry up. They were standing on the other side of the street, seemingly arguing about what carol to choose for Sebastian. Bernard felt himself sliding along the slippery hall tiles as the door began closing on him, despite using all his strength to keep it open. He desperately needed to stall Sebastian before he closed the door on him and the monkeys forever.

'Have you got their special skin sun cream though? They can't just use any old sun lotion,' said Bernard.

'They use sun lotion? Really?' said Sebastian, easing the pressure on the door.

'Yes, they have very delicate skin living under all that forest foliage,' said Bernard, managing to push the door a little wider as Sebastian pondered the use of sunscreen among monkeys.

'Oh, well, if you insist. My maid will make sure they get their special cream,' he said, pushing the door back an inch and then clicking his fingers.

As he turned to look for Larold, Bernard took advantage of Sebastian's lapse in concentration to squeeze through the door.

'It will only take a few minutes,' said Bernard as he kicked the door shut just in case Sebastian tried to physically eject him.

'It really isn't convenient. We have the Royal Variety Show rehearsals this evening...they're performing in front of the Queen tomorrow, don't you realise?' said Sebastian, reaching over Bernard to reopen the door.

'Yes, my invite seems to have been lost in the post.'

'No, sorry, Bernie. No can do. It's VIPs only. And anyway, if the monkeys see you they may get upset,' he spat.

'Upset?'

'Yes, you know this is their home now. We don't want to confuse them, do we?' he said, reaching out for the door handle.

'Er...I'm the one who's upset. I brought them up and trained them and now you're taking all the credit.'

'Oh really,' growled Sebastian. 'The cheek of it after all the money I've given you. You and those monkeys would be on the streets if it wasn't for me.'

But Bernard wasn't listening. Instead, he was trying to find the line of where Sebastian's wig was attached.

'It's good,' Bernard said. 'Very good.'

'What are you talking about, boy?'

'Oh, it's just good to be here,' said Bernard stepping away from the door towards the wide sweeping staircase where a giant portrait of Sebastian glowered over the hallway. 'To see Emile, Zola and Titus again. It's been a long, long time...and I've missed them so, so much,' said Bernard, launching himself at Sebastian and throwing his arms around his waist, pretending to sob.

Sebastian tried to push him away but Bernard clung onto his waist like the monkeys used to do to him.

'This...really...oh....please....your disgusting child oils...Oh, very well, you can see them for five minutes,' said Sebastian, desperately trying but failing to free himself from Bernard's hold.

Bernard immediately let go and Sebastian brushed himself down as if he'd split something revolting down his shirt.

'Larold, go and fetch the monkeys from the gara...I mean their playroom and take them into the sitting room,' he said, narrowing his eyes at Bernard. 'I'll be counting the seconds ,' he whispered.

Just then the doorbell rang.

'Shall I?' offered Bernard.

Without waiting for an answer, he opened the door to see the little girl he'd spoken to earlier standing on the steps, her mouth a perfect O of surprise as she saw Sebastian standing in the hallway. The rest of the carol singers stood behind her on the pavement below and after a cheery count of 1-2-3, they burst into *We Wish You a Merry Christmas.*

'No, no, no!' said Sebastian, scuttling up the stairs. 'Tell them there's no one here to give them money.'

'Sebastian said he'd love to hear you singing a whole medley of carols, so sing, sing, sing!' shouted Bernard, flinging the door open wide. 'Happy Christmas everyone!'

Realising he had several phones videoing him, Sebastian muttered a few bad words under his breath and slunk back down the stairs, a fixed smile adorning his face as he appeared at the door.

'Sorry! I've got an appointment with Her Maj...'

But he didn't manage to finish his sentence because Bernard shoved him onto the doorstep and slammed the door behind him. A few moments later, there came a terrific banging on the door followed by the doorbell ringing furiously, both accompanied by a rousing version of *Rudoph the Red Nosed Reindeer.*

Bernard turned to see Larold leading Emile, Zola and Titus along the hallway towards him. As soon as they saw him, they leapt on him, their little fingers locking around his neck.

'I've missed you so much,' said Bernard, tears rolling down his cheeks.

The monkeys chattered into his ears and kissed his face.

'Where's Sebastian?' asked Larold.

Bernard gestured to the door.

'The carol singers will keep him busy for another few minutes. I locked him out.'

She grinned and beckoned him into the sitting room before closing the door to drown out the sound of Sebastian's frantic knocking and bell ringing. Bernard peeled the monkeys' hands from him and sat them down on the sofa next to him as Larold found the video on her phone.

'You're not going to like what you're about to see but please believe me it's true,' Bernard said.

Larold played them the secret recording and the monkeys looked at one another, Titus scratching his quiff.

'I don't think they understand,' said Bernard. 'Show them the photo of Dr Wu.'

Then he turned to the monkeys and said: 'This is Sebastian's new friend who is coming to Barbados with you and Virgil. She's very bad.'

Larold clicked onto the search engine for images of Dr Wu and immediately a list of all Dr Wu branded products came up, including *Monkey Slow Painful Death Poison, Dancing Lemur You Got Rythm Potion, Tiger Power Powder, Black Bear Liver Remedy, Rhino Horn Moisturiser & Hangover Cure, Sleepy Sleepy Now!* and the even scarier *Sleepy Sleepy Forever!* and other despicable potions, using animal bones, organs, horns and tusks.

Larold clicked on another site and a photo of Dr Wu wearing a huge arctic fox fur coat popped up. Then came another of her smiling – that's if you could call baring a mouthful of little sharp piranha-like teeth - smiling. The monkeys jumped onto Bernard, covering their eyes with their little hands.

'Listen to this,' said Larold looking at the screen. 'She loves anything made out of animals but especially crocodile, snakes, guinea pigs and lemurs and under her hates – written in capitals...' said Larold sharing the image. 'Look! MONKEYS.'

Emile, Titus and Zola stared at the image of a tough-looking Barbary ape, the famous monkeys that inhabit the Rock of Gibraltar, presumably the same monkeys who had ruined Dr Wu's holiday. They looked up at Bernard and shrugged.

'I think I know what will make them understand,' Larold said, her eyes lighting up. 'But we don't have much time. Follow me.'

She flung open the door and they ran into the hall, past the almost continuous banging on the door, accompanying an anything but *Silent Night*. They scampered up the stairs to Sebastian's bedroom, all black satin sheets and velvet sofas with huge mirrors on nearly every wall, through to a massive dressing room, almost the same size as the bedroom, until they came to a closed door.

'I think this is where he keeps his wigs,' she explained. 'I followed him up here when I first came to stay and when he caught me, he gave me a really nasty Chinese burn and banned me from ever coming up here again.'

She twisted the door handle but it was locked.

'I'm pretty sure I saw him getting the key out of a shoe,' she said as they took in dozens of shelves stretching from floor to ceiling, stacked with hundreds of pairs of identical shiny black pointed shoes, all with a slight heel.

Bernard glanced at Larold. 'It's going to take ages to search through these, and, by the sounds of it, he's going to break the door down very soon,' he said.

'Not if we all search for it,' she said, pulling a key out of her pocket and showing it to the monkeys. 'We're looking for one of these, okay?'

Titus, Emile and Zola nodded.

'You do the top half,' she told them, 'and me and Bernard will do the lower half. Go!'

Within a few moments, Emile had double flipped back to the ground, holding the key out to Larold while bowing.

'Well done!' they clapped.

Larold fiddled around with the key, and then, at last, they heard the click of the lock and the door swung open.

Bernard's mouth also swung open as he took in the dozens of mannequin heads set on plinths lining the room, all wearing Sebastian's trademark quiff. But what was weirder still were hundreds of articles, scribblings and drawings glued to the walls, and others crumpled on the floor.

Bernard picked up a discarded drawing. It showed a pencil drawing of a robot named the *Monkey Snatcher* which used bananas on a pulley system to lure three badly drawn stick monkeys into a large net being held by a stick figure with a large quiff.

Bernard scooped up another ball of paper from the floor and unfolded it to reveal a stick man high up at a theatre with a large pair of scissors poised to cut through the rope of a trapeze swing where Emile, Zola and Titus were happily sitting.

He tossed the drawings aside and scanned articles about Dr Wu and her outrageous claims to cure baldness using a powder made from the bones of hairless monkeys. Bernard felt sick as he glanced at another wall and saw his own smiling face staring back at him. The wall was decorated with articles and pictures of Bernard and the monkeys and how much the public loved their acrobatic acts at Fluffingdale Farm.

Then, right next to the articles, were a series of diagrams showing how Sebastian planned to entice the monkeys from Bernard with promises of fame and fortune, exploit their talents to make millions and then kill them. Another diagram showed a picture of the monkeys with red Xs scrawled across their faces, next to a sinister picture of a scowling Dr Wu drinking from a monkey skull goblet.

The final picture was of Sebastian and Virgil smiling down at them, his quiff and Boghero's mullet labelled: BYE-BYE DISGUSTING MONKEYS AND ITCHY WIGS! HELLO TO REAL HAIR AT LAST!!!

As the monkeys took in the strange drawings and scrawlings of Sebastian, it eventually dawned on them what Sebastian had awaiting them in Barbados and they clung onto Bernard and Larold, their teeth chattering in fear.

'Let's get out of here, right now,' said Bernard.

'Er, no! Hold on a minute. That lets Sebastian and Virgil off far too lightly. They need to be punished for what they're planning,' said Larold.

'Well, we can do that without putting Titus, Emile and Zola at risk. There's no way I'm letting them stay another minute with that psycho.'

'But, Bernard, think about it. If he knows we've uncovered his secret, he'll never let any of you leave. We could all be in danger,' said Larold, quickly relocking the door and throwing the key up into a shoe on the top shelf.

Bernard's stomach flipped for the millionth time that day.

'No way,' he said pushing past Larold with the monkeys all

riding on his back. 'You can stay here if you like but we're off. He doesn't scare me.'

Bernard felt himself being spun round to face Larold as she grabbed his arm. She then grasped both his wrists tightly.

'Oh, thanks. So you'll leave me here to face him alone?' she said, tears beginning to pool.

He tried to pull his arms away but her grip was surprisingly strong.

'No, of course not. You're coming with us.'

'And you think he'll let us just leave like that,' said Larold. 'Leave us and the monkeys alone? We've uncovered your evil plan and now we're going. Bye!' said Larold, mimicking Bernard.

'There's no need to be like that,' he said, finally freeing his wrists from her grip.

'You don't know what he's capable of. He'll come after you. He always gets what he wants which is why we need to stop him.'

Just then, they all turned to look down the stairs as the front door shuddered loudly.

'LET ME IN!' Sebastian shouted before adding in a polite voice: 'Don't forget, Larold dear. We have an important date with the Queen tomorrow. I need my beauty sleep.'

Larold grabbed Bernard's wrist again.

'Listen to me. I've got a plan. We can get rid of Sebastian forever and be safe.'

Bernard yanked his arm away.

'No, way. We're going and if you want to come, come, but don't drag me and the monkeys into your stupid plan.'

'He won't let you take them, Bernard.'

'We'll go to the police. They'll help us.'

'And say what? That the most famous man in the UK is about to kill the most popular monkeys in the world? Who are they going to believe? A couple of kids or a famous TV star?'

Bernard stamped his foot.

'But they'll be too scared to stay here now. If they don't do what he says for the performance tomorrow, then Sebastian may kill them straight away.'

'No, trust me. It won't happen. He has too much riding on the performance. Anyway, he leaves the monkeys with me all the time. He doesn't have anything to do with them unless he's showing off in front of his friends. Listen, Bernard,' she pleaded. 'I've got it all worked out if only you'll let them stay and we can all have revenge,' said Larold, reaching up to stroke Titus' quiff.

'Hang on a moment, how do I know you're not in on his plan too?' said Bernard, suspiciously.

Larold rolled her eyes. 'Why would I warn you? It makes no sense.'

Bernard shrugged. It was true. It didn't make sense. But then nothing made sense any more. He couldn't think straight with the singing and Sebastian bashing at the door and demanding to be let in, and now the monkeys were chattering away to one another right in his ears.

'But they don't understand what revenge is. It would be mine and yours' revenge, not theirs,' said Bernard as Titus peeled himself off him and his sister and brother jumped to the floor.

The monkeys held hands and jumped onto the banister

where they pointed to a picture of Sebastian and Virgil at the opening of *Snazzle Dazzle* and drew a line with their fingers across Sebastian's throat. They then leapt onto Bernard and gave him a kiss before jumping onto Larold.

'See! They do understand. I promise you, Bernard. I would never let anything bad happen to them. You'll be at the show anyway, so you can intervene any time,' she said.

'Er...no, I can't because I haven't been invited,' said Bernard. 'Sebastian said it was VIPs only and too upsetting for the monkeys for me to be there.'

'Oh, did he now? But I've got the guest list,' she smiled. 'I'll put you, Ryan and Brenda on with full backstage access.'

Chapter 17

Bernard battled to keep the images of Sebastian's mad scribblings out of his head as he walked back to the Underground.

However, he couldn't erase the image of Sebastian turning to look at him as he opened the front door. The hairs on the back of his neck stood up when he recalled how his amber eyes burnt into him as they followed him along the street. Bernard was just thankful that the carol singers had grouped around him for photos, trapping Sebastian on the steps.

Now he was away from the monkeys, Larold's promise to make sure Sebastian would pay for his evil plan, and keep them out of their lives forever, suddenly seemed highly unlikely.

Who was she kidding? They were *his* precious monkeys, no-one else's. Yet everyone seemed to think they knew what was best for them. Why had he left them there? He must be mad, he realised.

He raced back up the Underground's steep steps, oblivious to the passers-by tutting at him as he knocked into them. Then, at the top of the stairs, he remembered how Emile, Titus and Zola had made the violent gesture at Sebastian and Virgil's photo hanging on the staircase and he reluctantly turned and retraced his steps into the underground station. When he reached the train station, he stopped on the platform unable to step into the carriage, again questioning whether the monkeys really understood what revenge was.

He vaguely remembered his mother telling him that chimpanzees in zoos often wreak revenge on other chimps for stealing food, and Ryan had once told him about vengeful dairy cows, who attacked farmers for taking away their new born calves. He recalled how the monkeys often ganged up on each other if one of them stole sweets or their share of asparagus.

'The Star Wars Millennium Falcon wee incident!' Bernard said aloud, just as a couple with their two teenage children walked past, giving him a wide berth.

Bernard blushed, jumped onto the carriage and huddled in the far corner. He remembered how Zola had weed all over the spaceship after Titus and Emile had broken her favourite keyboard. He'd painstakingly taken apart the spaceship brick by brick, washed each one and then rebuilt it. There was no doubt they understood the concept of revenge.

But would they be able to enact it before Sebastian had a chance to whisk them away to Barbados where the evil Dr Wu was waiting to chop them into Lego-sized pieces? He took in a deep breath and tried to breath out all his negative thoughts of what could go wrong, slowly coming to the realisation that he'd just have to trust Larold.

By the time the train had pulled into Fluffingdale, Bernard was feeling a little calmer: Larold had texted him 29 times, assuring him that the monkeys would be safe with her and that his name was on the Royal Variety's guest list with Ryan's and Brenda's.

And as he reached the house, he received another: *At the-atre. Rehearsal for Operation Revenge complete. No need to worry. Please don't ring or text. S is suspicious after looking for key to wig room. Says it wasn't where it should have been. See you tom.*

Oh, God, please don't let Sebastian hurt them, repeated Bernard over and over again as he walked back to the house. Then he began to feel hypocritical because he wasn't a bit religious and wondered if he should in fact be praying to the god of hairless monkeys. *Whoever you are, oh, great Hairless Monkey God of the Amazon, save your brothers and sisters who are in mortal danger from Sebastian, Boghero and Dr Wu. Please, please save them*, repeated Bernard over and over again until he reached the house.

Then as he put the key in the door, Bernard began to fret that if a great Hairless Monkey God did exist, then he may have angered it by not making an offering. But what kind of offering should he make? Palm hearts and acai berries or gold and diamonds?

Bernard felt as if his head would explode with all the appeasing hairless monkey gods' scenarios and was relieved to hear Armando and Loki racing along the hallway to greet him as he opened the door.

He knelt down and hugged Armando while sinking his face into Loki's luxuriant fur, feeling that perhaps things were going to be okay after all.

Chapter 18

'What a treat, Bernard, inviting us to see Emile, Titus and Zola perform in front of the Queen,' said Brenda.

They were being shown to their seats in the grand theatre, just two rows from the stage. Bernard glanced around at all the guests arriving, thinking how the men looked like a colony of penguins in white shirts and black dinner jackets, and the ladies like exotic birds showing off their fine feathers.

As soon as they sat down, Brenda opened her glittery handbag and took out several bulging paper bags.

'Thought I'd go for a mixture of all your favourites, rhubarb and custard, pear drops, strawberry bon bons for me and some love hearts for you, Ryan,' she said arching her eyebrows and offering one of the sweets to Ryan.

He took one and blushed.

Bernard tried to smother his smile as he read the caption on the sweet *'TRUE LOVE'* before it disappeared into Ryan's mouth. Brenda offered the bag of bon bons to Bernard.

'No thanks, I feel bit queasy,' he replied.

'I'm not surprised,' said Ryan. 'I'm nervous for you, Bernard. To think of Emile, Zola and Titus performing in front of all these VIPs.'

'Like us,' Brenda joked before glancing around and adding, 'Though they're a very glamorous lot.'

'You look just as glamorous,' said Ryan, crunching on his sweet.

It was now Brenda's turn to blush.

'Oh, don't be silly,' she said.

'No, it's true. You look lovely,' said Bernard, admiring Brenda's sparkly blue dress.

Although she may not have spent thousands of pounds on a dress and shoes like the famous celebrities filling the seats, Brenda looked every bit as beautiful in her dress with her dark hair swept up in a bun.

'And you look a treat in your ironed clothes, Bernard. I bet they got a shock of their life, never having been near an iron before,' she said.

'Mmm,' said Bernard as he looked down at his favourite jeans which now looked brand new with the sharp crease down the middle.

'And you don't scrub up so badly either, Ryan,' said Brenda, sending him into a mini coughing fit.

Ryan was spared any more embarrassment by the lights dimming and the roll of drums.

'Ladies and gentlemen, please rise for Her Majesty the Queen,' a deep voice boomed from the theatre speakers.

Everyone then stood and clapped as the Queen came into her Royal box with various attendants and nodded and waved before sitting.

'Ooh, she's got her crown on and all,' whispered Brenda.

As they sat down again, the lights went back on briefly, and Bernard felt his heart race as he saw Sebastian and Virgil rushing to take their seats in the front row to his left. Larold had told him that Sebastian would be backstage but here he was right in front of him. If Sebastian saw him, he'd probably have him thrown out.

'Oh, look it's Sebastian, Bernard,' said Brenda, elbowing him.

Bernard slunk low in his seat, hiding his face behind the programme.

'Aren't you going to say hello?'

'No!' squeaked Bernard.

'I thought you'd want to let him know you're here,' she added.

'I'll speak to him after the show,' said Bernard, now regretting his decision not to tell them what was going on. He'd wanted to tell them on the way in the car, but they were chatting away so much, there hadn't been a good time to interrupt. To be honest, he'd felt like a big fat gooseberry and, for most of the journey, sat staring out the window praying to the God of Hairless Monkeys to protect Emile, Titus and Zola from the evil Sebastian.

Then, outside the theatre, he was about to tell them, when Brenda spotted several actors from her favourite soap, *Bouffant Bay*, going into the theatre and ran after them for autographs.

'Are you all right?' whispered Ryan.

Bernard nodded. 'Just a bit nervous.'

'It's a shame he doesn't know you're here...I can get his attention if you like,' continued Brenda, leaning forward and peering at the back of Sebastian's head.

'I'll have those sweets now,' Bernard said, trying to distract her by dipping his hand into her handbag and then stuffing several pear drops into his mouth.

'Is that a good idea if you're feeling sick?' asked Ryan as the lights dimmed.

Bernard didn't have time to answer because the same deep voice boomed across the theatre.

'Ladies and gentlemen, your Royal Highness, the Queen. Welcome to the London Palladium for the Royal Variety Performance. And here's your host, Johnnneeeeeeeee Golden.'

The audience clapped as the curtains parted to reveal a middle-aged man wearing a shiny green suit and a head of greasy dyed black hair. He grabbed the microphone and launched into several gags. Bernard tried to concentrate on the jokes but his mind kept wandering, worrying where Emile, Zola and Titus were and whether they were safe. He watched the audience laughing as the host pranced up and down the front row. His suit was stretched so tightly over his large paunch that Bernard hoped the shiny buttons would shoot into the audience and hit Sebastian and Virgil's murderous faces.

Then the first act came on, the cast of a West End musical. Athough Bernard didn't catch the name of the hit show, he thought it may have something to do with cats because their singing sounded just like felines yowling and fighting.

Next up was a magician called The Great Dave who Bernard had seen on TV a couple of times.

'Ooh, I like him,' said Brenda.

Bernard's legs started jiggling around.

'Do you need the toilet, Bernard?' asked Ryan.

'I'm not a toddler,' snapped Bernard. He was really fond

of Ryan but sometimes it felt like he treated him like the tiny child he'd known when he used to work with his dad.

'Are you ready for some magic?' asked The Great Dave.

Bernard sat up as he watched him walk over to Sebastian and gestured for him to join him on stage to riotous applause. He knew magicians sometimes cut people in half. He hoped the same fate awaited Sebastian. But that something would go terribly wrong and he would actually cut him in half.

'Now we all know that you're famed for your shock of ginger hair, Sebastian. So how do you feel if we give it a cut?'

Sebastian backed away and threw his hands up in mock horror.

'No! Anything but my hair!'

'You big fat fake!' Bernard blurted out.

Brenda looked at him sharply.

'Oh, Bernard. He's a magician. It's meant to be fake, isn't it?'

'No, I meant Sebastian,' said Bernard.

'That's a bit harsh. What with all he's done for you and the monkeys.'

'I wasn't sure about him before, to be honest,' whispered Ryan, 'but the newspapers were full of photos of him posing with carol singers after they'd knocked on his door and he'd come out into the street to listen. Can't be that bad?'

Bernard felt his face flushing as he tried to quell the urge to shout: *Only because I locked him out of his house!*

'I think we've all had enough of Sebastian, don't you?' the magician asked the audience, who roared with delight along with Bernard.

The Great Dave bundled Sebastian into a metal upright

box and closed the door. He then spun the box around so that the audience could just see Sebastian's head poking out. He clicked his fingers and two burly men came on stage, took hold of the box and lay it on a low metal table face up. The Great Dave spun the box round again asking: 'How you feeling, Sebastian?'

'A little dizzy,' came a muffled reply.

'Ready for a haircut?'

'No, please! Not my hair!' said Sebastian in exaggerated horror.

'Now this hair cut, ladies and gentlemen, is slightly different from your average trip to the barbers,' he said, pulling out a huge shiny, sharp blade from a metal box on the floor. 'Heard of the guillotine, Sebastian?'

Bernard was pleased to see a look of real fear flashing across Sebastian's orange face.

'Yes, the French were fond of these. Oops, no offence, Your Majesty,' added The Great Dave, nodding to the Queen in her Royal Box.

'Well, when I said haircut. I may have been underestimating just how much I was going to cut off.'

'What?' said Sebastian, panicked.

'Byeeee!' said The Great Dave as he pulled up a metal gate over Sebastian's face.

The audience gasped as he sliced the guillotine right through Sebastian's neck. He then pulled the box apart separating Sebastian's head from his body with The Great Dave standing between the two.

'Comfortable?' asked Dave.

'A little disconnected,' said Sebastian.

'Oh, dear! I hope he's all right. It looks ever so realistic,' whispered Brenda, shovelling a handful of lemon bon bons into her mouth.

'Please don't put him back together again,' Bernard muttered.

Perhaps this was Larold's great plan, he wondered. While Sebastian was trapped in the box, she'd slip out with the monkeys.

But after spinning the boxes several times, The Great Dave set about doing just the opposite of what Bernard wanted. After it came to a rest, Sebastian stepped out of the box onto the stage, head and neck firmly on his shoulders.

'I hate you Sebastian Trophy-Assetclass,' spat Bernard.

Ryan and Brenda stared at Bernard in puzzlement.

'You didn't even let them come to the opening of the zoo. They would have loved it,' he said, grabbing some more rhubarb and custards, oblivious to his two companions exchanging concerned glances.

In fact, Bernard was so caught up in his crossness and sweet scoffing that he hadn't noticed that The Great Dave had left the stage and the curtain was opening slowly to reveal Titus, Emile and Zola swinging on three trapezes, across a jungle scene of giant trees, sprouting monster purple and orange flowers and lurid green leaves.

'Bernard, love,' said Brenda, elbowing him. 'They're on.'

'Now we have a real treat for you,' said Johnny Golden, who was back on the stage. 'They're in the middle of their European tour but they've taken time out to be here today. Put your hands together for Sebastian Trophy-Assetclass's amazing, fabulous, incredible, death-defying, breathtaking monkeeeeeeeeeeeee showwww staring Ding, Dang and Donnnnnnnng!'

Bernard glanced around at Brenda and Ryan and the rest of the audience, his mouth hanging open. *Sebastian Trophy-Assetclass's amazing, fabulous, incredible, death-defying, breathtaking hairless monkey show.*

They're my words, bristled Bernard. Not only has he stolen my monkeys but my words too!

Bernard watched transfixed as the monkeys sailed through the air from trapeze to trapeze. As they flew across the stage, the audience gasped in delight and horror and he suddenly noticed why. There was no safety net just as Sebastian's mad scribbling had indicated. Bernard sat up, terrified that Sebastian had changed his plan and was going to kill the monkeys now. Would he have to jump out of his seat and onto the stage to stop the show? He desperately scanned the top of the set to see if Virgil Boghero was poised with a large pair of scissors, then peered over at the front row, relieved to see him sitting with Sebastian.

'Don't worry, Bernard,' whispered Ryan. 'They live in the tallest trees in the world. Hairless monkeys don't do falling from great heights.'

Bernard's stomach began to somersault again as much as the monkeys as he watched them through his fingers. Emile hung onto Zola who held onto Titus, who in turn swung from one of the trapezes. The trapeze then swung higher and higher until Zola reached the far trapeze and jumped on safely. Then Emile did the same. Titus jumped from his trapeze, somersaulting and twisting through the air to land perfectly on his feet. Emile followed, landing on Titus's shoulders and finally Zola leapt from her trapeze, spinning through the air, gracefully landing on Emile's shoulders to riotous applause.

They then performed a series of daring leaps and jumps from trampoline to trampoline finishing with Zola playing Queen's *Bohemian Rhapsidy* while balancing on Titus's head. The applause grew louder as Sebastian walked onto the stage bowing to the audience, some of whom were giving him a standing ovation.

'The cheeky devil,' said Ryan. 'It's as if he was the one who'd just performed the whole show.'

'That's near enough their old routine. He's hardly changed a thing. All them times he told you they were practising,' said Brenda, shaking her head. 'Shame on him.'

Bernard grimaced as he held back the urge to retch. When exactly was Larold going to save them? Maybe, if he stood up now and told everyone about Sebastian's despicable plan, he could rescue them? But his heart was thundering so loudly, he couldn't think clearly. His mouth felt dry and his legs had turned into two useless wobbly jellies. A combination of nerves and too many sweets had made him feel so sick that he didn't know what to do with himself. All he could do was watch as Sebastian bowed extravagantly to the Queen, while Emile, Zola, and Titus raced over to join him.

Bernard then noticed that the monkeys, who usually loved to pose and bow for ages in front of their audiences, were trying to climb up Sebastian. But Sebastian kept playfully pushing them away while smiling at the audience. Bernard saw Zola glancing over to the side of the stage and, after a few moments, jumped off Sebastian and scampered to the back where she shimmied up a tree and sprung onto a trapeze. Bernard's heart nearly stopped as he watched Zola swinging higher and higher. He nudged his companions. But, like the rest of the audience, they were entranced by Sebastian's comic battle to keep Emile and Titus from climbing on him, and hadn't spotted Zola.

'Look!' said Bernard, pointing to the top of the stage.

As if on cue, Zola flew off the trapeze, somersaulted through the air, landing on Sebastian's back. He stumbled forwards a few steps and Zola swiped at his quiff, knocking it slightly askew. Quickly regaining his balance, Sebastian managed to massage his quiff back into place with Emile and Titus holding tightly around his waist. At the same time, Zola wrapped her legs around Sebastian's neck, rolled back and pushed up, her fingers poised over his wig.

Sebastian, who must have guessed what was about to happen, screamed at the top of his voice.

'GET YOUR DISGUSTING MONKEY FINGERS AWAY FROM MY BEAUTIFUL HAIR!'

A hush descended upon the audience as Sebastian, who realised his real opinion of the monkeys had just been broadcast to 20 million viewers, flung his hands over his mouth.

Zola then plucked the wig from his head, spun it round and round to gain momentum and threw it high across the audience. The camera followed the famous orange flame whizzing through the air like a comet before landing on top of Her Majesty's crown.

Bernard felt the bile rising up and couldn't swallow it back this time. He pushed past his guests, desperate to get to the toilets, but it was too late. He lurched forward and a liquid mush of regurgitated pear drops and rhubarb and custards spewed over Virgil Boghero's greasy grey mullet.

Chapter 19

Bernard and the monkeys arrived safely home in the early hours of the morning, accompanied by The Great Dave and Larold.

'Me and Sebastian go way back,' The Great Dave explained while Bernard made everyone mugs of hot chocolate.

'We worked as Redcoats at a holiday camp in the 1980s and I'd say he was the best friend I ever had. That's until he stole the floating bunny act and claimed it as his own.'

'The floating bunny act was yours?' Bernard gasped.

'Oh, yes, I'd spent two whole years perfecting that act. As a rule, us magicians don't tell each other our special tricks, but I thought Sebastian was my best friend. We did everything together. We were like brothers. He knew I was working on a groundbreaking act with rabbits but I'd been vague about the details and that was fine, that's how us magicians work. A strictly need to know relationship, if you get my drift?'

Bernard, rendered speechless by the depth of Sebastian's deceit, nodded and The Great Dave continued with his tale of treachery.

'Well, one night we were in the pub and he plied me with super-strength cider to loosen my tongue. I was young and I just couldn't help myself from boasting about how I'd managed to get the bunnies to float and before I knew it, I was in my kitchen giving him a one man show. The next thing I know he gets a slot on that kid's TV show and he's refusing to take my calls.'

'And he becomes a big star,' said Bernard, finding his tongue again.

'And muggins here is still performing at the local clubs.'

'But you could have carried on doing the act?' Bernard said.

'No, I couldn't. You see, he stole my bunnies too that night, all 20 of them. I worked out pretty quickly he'd taken them but he denied any knowledge,' explained The Great Dave, wiping away a stray tear rolling down his cheek. 'They were like my babies. I'd hand-reared them and had spent eighteen months training them. All for nothing.'

'And that's what he did to me and the monkeys!' said Bernard.

'I know. When I saw them on *Fame Me!* I knew straight away he was up to his old tricks again. So I was more than happy to help Larold when she asked. You see, me and Larold's mum go way back, so she knew about my hatred of Sebastian. We had it all planned. While I worked on flattering Sebastian - as much as it pained me - to get him to agree to be in my act, Larold worked with Emile, Zola and Titus getting them to follow her instructions. When the monkeys came running into the wings, we hid them in my magic boxes. I think Sebastian knew they were in there but he couldn't work out how to open them. He always was a rubbish magician.'

'It was pretty scary, Bernard. I could hear him ranting and

raving about what he was going to do to us when he caught us!' said Larold.

'I bet,' said Bernard.

'I took great pleasure in watching him searching behind curtains, down trap doors, under piles of discarded costumes and trying to open my boxes, all the while threatening me with lawsuits,' said The Great Dave. 'Then the police arrived and he was escorted out of the stage door where the world's paparazzi were waiting.'

'Oh, I wish I'd seen his face,' said Bernard.

'It was brilliant. And I'll tell you what else is brilliant, Bernard. Them monkeys. Bright as buttons, they are. They followed Larold's instructions to the book.'

'Except for flinging his stupid wig at the Queen,' said Larold.

'Well, in the eyes of the law, Sebastian is meant to have them under his control. It's about time he got his comeuppance,' said The Great Dave who finished off his cocoa. 'And it's time for me to go. I've promised my wife I'd be home in time for breakfast.'

'Are you coming with me, Larold? You're very welcome. We've got a comfy sofa you can have,' added The Great Dave.

Larold shrugged. 'I hadn't really thought about where I'd go...I was waiting for my mum to pick me up.'

'Oh, she's come back? Is she picking you up from here then?' asked Bernard, feeling disappointed that Larold would be leaving so quickly.

He'd only known her for a short time but it'd been nice to have someone his own age to hang around with.

'Say hello to your mum from me,' said The Great Dave as

they walked him to the door. 'Any problems then you know where to find me.'

After thanking The Great Dave once again, Bernard closed the door behind him. 'So what time's your mum coming?' he asked.

'Well, not any time soon - I've been waiting two years.'

'Two years? What about your dad?'

'What about him? He dumped me at Sebastian's when he went off with his new girlfriend.'

'Well, haven't you got anyone else in your family. Any grandparents, or other aunts or uncles, cousins?'

Larold shook her head, her cheerful, lively curls at odds with the sad look that came over her. He realised she was the same as him. All alone in the world. Both his parents had been only children and his grandparents had died when he was a five.

'And school?'

'Sebastian said he was far too busy for me to go to school and I'd learn more sticking with him. Learn more about cooking and cleaning, I think he meant. But don't worry about me. I can look after myself.'

'But how old you are?'

'Twelve in three months.'

'So you're only eleven?'

'Nearly twelve,' she said, standing straight.

'Well, nearly twelve still isn't old enough to look after yourself.'

'You can hardly talk.'

'But the difference is that you don't have anywhere to stay,' he said. 'So I think you should stay here for now...that's...if you'd like to?' he asked, hesitantly.

Larold glanced around at the huge hallway as if taking in the enormity of the house for the first time.

'If you're sure you can squeeze me in, I suppose I could stay for a couple of weeks,' said Larold, grinning.

Chapter 20

And so it was that Larold's 'just a couple of weeks' stretched until the cherry tree blossom transformed the overgrown lawn into a pink carpet.

Up to this point, they spent most of their time at the zoo where Larold took a particular liking to Mr Stripey and Marley, the Bunny-eating tigers. It was a liking that Bernard and the zoo keepers were pleased to see was mutual. The tigers no longer hung around at the back of their jungle area, hiding in their new cave or skulking behind trees. Instead they started to venture out to where the visitors could see them. And by the end of spring, Larold had taken over the role as unofficial Head Tiger Keeper, much to the relief of all the zookeepers, who had been drawing daily straws at feeding time.

The number of visitors during the winter had naturally fallen but once the monkeys had overseen the design and build of a new performance arena, numbers dramatically increased. Bookings sold out quickly and the zoo began to make a small but steady profit. However, Bernard didn't need to worry about the zoo making money any more thanks to a generous donation from Sebastian.

After the Queen decided to drop the assault charge, he'd fled London to his Barbadian retreat. Larold had then emailed her uncle informing him that if he'd been looking for all the diagrams and drawings in his wig room, then not to worry. She would keep them away from the media, just as long as he made a big fat contribution to the zoo. Of £5 million. And never bothered her, Bernard and the monkeys ever again.

Life couldn't have been sweeter for all of them. Well, when I say all of them, I may be exaggerating. Because although the monkeys were delighted not to have been turned into a quack cure for baldness, they were somewhat annoyed to have two very furry rivals to share Bernard with. And equally, Loki and Armando, never having lived with the monkeys, were not natural sharers of affection.

Reader, let's just say that certain animals do not mix well as Bernard and Larold were to find out. The monkeys were used to being the centre of attention wherever they went. Their fans travelled from as far as Chile and China just to catch a glimpse of them performing their death-defying acrobatics. And as far as they were concerned, they still saw themselves as the apple of Bernard's eye. They were his babies first and foremost, and as far as they were concerned, Loki and Armando could go away and go back to doing all the cat and anteatery things they'd been doing before Bernard had rescued them.

At first, Emile, Zola and Titus tried to show the newcomers who was boss. This usually took the form of ambushing Armando and Loki when they were sleeping, and locking them in dark cupboards, until Bernard or Larold were alerted by Loki's plaintive mewing and Armando's strange grunting. But gradually, Armando and Loki learnt to fight back. Bernard treated the monkeys' bites and scratches with lots of antiseptic cream but little sympathy. And after each attack,

Bernard would attempt to make peace between the creatures, trying to entice the monkeys to say hello to Armando and Loki. He'd run his fingers through their coats as if the possession of fur somehow made them the better creatures.

'Look how soft it is. Come and feel,' he'd say although, to be honest, he'd skim his hand over Armando's bristly coat.

The monkeys learnt to keep their distance, becoming wary of Armando's claws which he took to examining every time they came near, and Loki's razor-like claws which sprung out like flick knives every time they dared to look his way.

'You will just have to tolerate one another,' Bernard told them one night, kissing the monkeys good night, while he disappeared into his bedroom with a very smug-looking Armando and Loki glancing back at them.

It was during this time that Bernard began to dream about his parents for the first time since their deaths. They often appeared at foot of his bed, smiling at him, and when he woke, he wondered what the dream had meant. Had they forgiven him? Had saving all the animals, including the monkeys, somehow cancelled out his badness and he was free to start his life again?

And, as he went downstairs to make a cup of tea one morning after one such dream, he kept thinking that perhaps, just perhaps, he could finally allow himself to be just a teeny tiny bit happy.

Chapter 21

But, as we all know, reader, nothing in life ever remains the same. Six months of relative calm at Fluffingdale began to fall apart that very morning.

'Did you...see that, Larold?' Bernard asked, jumping up and peering out of the window into the garden.

Bernard blinked several times, wondering if he was seeing things. He'd been eating breakfast at the time, listening to a fat robin singing on the windowsill, contemplating why birds always looked like they were complaining while singing so beautifully, when what kind only be described as a raggedy beast galloped past.

'What?' she said absentmindedly, staring at her phone.

'Oh, nothing,' he said, realising that Larold didn't take any notice of anything unless it was on her phone or was tiger-shaped.

And anyway, he wasn't sure what he'd actually seen.

'Must have been something,' she mumbled vaguely, looking up. 'What was it?'

'I'm not really sure. Some kind of strange creature.'

'Probably just the monkeys messing around,' she said, looking back at her phone.

'I wouldn't have thought so. They're still in bed, resting from practising.'

He watched Larold stand and roll her eyes at him.

'What's that for?'

'Nothing,' she said, walking to the window and looking out. 'I saw them messing around outside early morning yesterday, that's all.'

'This was definitely not anything monkey-like. For a start it had lots of fur...well, patchy fur at least, though it looked as if it had some kind of skin condition like the foxes, mange or something.'

'It's probably one of those things you get wool from. Maybe it escaped mid-shave,' said Larold, slumping back in her chair as if exhausted from the walk to the window and back.

'One of those things you get wool from that's escaped mid-shave?' repeated Bernard, shaking his head in despair. 'I think you mean a sheep, and they don't shave them,' said Bernard. 'They shear them.'

'Same thing.'

'Not,' muttered Bernard. 'For a start they don't use shaving foam or a razor.'

'And?' said Larold, still staring at her phone.

Bernard tutted and looked out at the window, marvelling at her stupidity about animals. But then, he immediately felt guilty. His parents had been conservationists and explorers. The house was full of books about all the wonderful creatures in the world. She clearly hadn't grown up around animals or in the countryside like him. Bernard thought she may have mentioned that she'd grown up in London but thinking about it, he didn't actually know.

In fact, he didn't really know an awful lot about her. He'd tried to ask but every time he'd done so, she'd say she didn't want to talk about it and then turn the question on him. He realised he knew no more about her than she liked Jaffa Cakes, tigers and spent a lot of time reading things on her phone. Perhaps it was time for another try.

'Do you ever wonder where your parents are?' he asked, tentatively.

'I've told you this already, Bernard,' she said, impatiently. 'My Mum left me and my Dad, and he cared more about gallivanting around with his girlfriends, so why should I be interested in them?'

'I just thought you may be curious about where they were, especially your mu...'

'Well, I could say the same about you,' she interrupted, looking up from her phone at last. 'Aren't you ever curious to find out what really happened to your parents?'

'I know what happened. I was there, thank you. They died in a hot air ballooning accident,' said Bernard, his voice becoming choked.

'Yeah, but was it really...an accident?' she said, placing her phone on her lap. 'And why have you turned all their photos to face the wall,' she added, springing up from her seat and grabbing one off the mantelpiece.

She turned it to face him. It was a photo of Bernard with a baby elephant at the elephant orphanage in Zambia.

'Put that down,' said Bernard, trying to snatch it from her.

'What are you scared of, Bernard? Why don't you want to

be reminded of them?' she replied, hiding the photo behind her back.

'Give it back.'

'No,' she said, running to the other side of the room. 'Let me look at it. It's cute. Where was it taken?'

'Why are you so interested? Just give it back,' said Bernard, feeling his face reddening. 'I said GIVE IT BACK!'

'All right, Mr Angry. I'm just interested.'

'If I tell you, will you give it back?'

'I suppose.'

'An orphanage where the babies go when their mums are killed by the poachers...those are the ones lucky enough to survive without their mums. Now give it back,' said Bernard, swiping it out of Larold's hands.

'There's no need to be like that,' said Larold, slumping back in her chair. 'I was just making conversation. I mean you never talk about your parents and how they died. It was a big mystery at the time, I remember seeing it on the news.'

'What are you talking about? It was an accident,' said Bernard, placing the photo frame back on the mantelpiece, round the wrong way again.

Bernard turned to see Larold's cheeks colouring. She began squirming in her seat and picked up her phone, scrolling down at something again.

'Well, I just remember it being on the TV. They said it was suspicious, that there were... question marks.'

'What question marks? And who are 'they'?' asked Bernard, aware of an awful sinking feeling.

Did Larold know their deaths had been his fault? And if so, how on earth did she find out?

'Well, they weren't sure how... it happened, that's all,' said Larold, avoiding looking at Bernard and gazing into the garden.

'How it happened? I'll tell you how it happened, shall I? You can hear about it firsthand instead of listening to all those stupid rumours. The gas exploded and the balloon fell to earth. End of story. I don't need you to tell me how my parents died,' said Bernard.

'But how did the gas explode, Bernard? Were you never curious to find out?' Larold asked, turning to look at him.

Bernard felt the anger coursing through his veins. How dare she churn up the past? The searing pain of what happened had inhabited every bone, muscle and pore for over three years, gradually fading into a constant dull ache in his chest. He thought he'd managed to bury the raw hurt inside but realised that his grief was like a scab that never heals, one that his supposed friend was now picking away at.

'You're as bad as Armando, sticking your nose in where it's not wanted.'

'Sorreeee,' said Larold. 'But I could say the same about you. Always trying to wheedle information out of me about my parents.'

'You make me sound like I wee over everything. I do not wheedle whatever that means.'

'You do! *Oh, Larold, I don't mean to be nosey but what happened to your mother and your father,*' mimicked Larold.

'I'm just interested.'

'Nosey-parker.'

'You're the nosey-parker!'

'Wheedler.'

'I do not wheedle.'

'Do.'

'Not.'

'Do, do, do, do.'

'Don't, don't, don't.'

Reader, I think you will be familiar with this tedious squabble. You see, Bernard and Larold, despite being remarkable children, were just that. Children. So if you have some homework to do, or need to tidy your room, or even make a nice cup of tea for your mum or dad, now is a very good time to do it.

Ten minutes later, with both squabblers refusing to give ground and let the other have the last word, they were very relieved to hear the office phone ring.

'Yes?' said Bernard, snatching it up.

'Oh Bernard, love, something very mysterious is happening to the zoo animals,' said the familiar voice of Brenda. 'You need to come straight away. Best leave the monkeys, Loki and Armando at home, just in case.'

Chapter 22

On the way to the zoo, Bernard felt little prickles of annoyance running over him whenever he thought of his conversation with Larold. He'd made her stay at the house to keep an eye on the monkeys because relations between Loki and Armando and the monkeys had completely broken down.

As he went to get dressed, he'd come across Armando thrashing around in the hallway downstairs, his nose jammed into the vacuum cleaner's extension tube. Normally, he would have blamed the incident on Armando's natural curiosity. However, Bernard had hoovered the house the day before and remembered putting the hoover away in the cupboard and securing the door catch. Armando could do a lot of amazing things like sniff out an ant nest from several hundred metres, and speedily sweep up the picnic area after littering visitors, but he could not open doors.

Therefore, Bernard concluded someone must have deliberately placed the extension tube over his nose. And the only creatures capable of doing such a thing would be Larold, or the monkeys. As Larold had no quarrel with Armando, as far as he knew, it was a fair assumption that the monkeys had been responsible. Just as they were probably responsible for squirting glue and glitter over Loki's fur several days before, and trying to glue Armando's super long tongue to the wall the week before.

Bernard took out his *Anteaters Rule!* Annual from his bag and tried reading. But he couldn't concentrate. The words became a jumble of meaningless marks jumping around on the page as all his worries begged for attention. The broken truce between Armando and Loki and the monkeys was the least of his concerns. He had never heard the normally laid-back Brenda sound so alarmed and he was terrified as to what awaited him.

But the biggest worry of all was what Larold had said earlier. It kept muscling all the other worries out of the way, demanding to be heard.

But how did the gas explode, Bernard? Were you never curious to find out?

And then all the memories of his parents' deaths came flooding back, how he'd had to fly home with the kind lady from the embassy who smelt of roses and kept feeding him boiled sweets and pitying smiles. How the repulsive Ms Snodgeweed had been waiting at the airport and gave him a brief, awkward hug, before telling him to hurry up and stop dawdling otherwise she'd miss the semi-finals of *Fame Me!* It'd all been a blur at the time. Looking after the monkeys every day and then taking over the zoo had helped him to block out the memories. But now Larold had dragged it all back up.

Bernard stifled his tears as dozens of memories began to bombard him, leading him down one particular path he'd avoided going down ever since the inquest. He'd told everyone that he hadn't been able to go on the balloon trip because he'd had a stomach upset. But the truth was that Bernard had been a big fat coward. A wave of fear had overcome him and he'd thrown himself over the side to the ground, just as the balloon was taking off. He'd been too scared to tell his parents he was afraid of extreme heights, ever since a school trip to the Eiffel Tower had left him shaking and vomiting. As he fell to the ground, the balloon had swayed from side to side dangerously.

He closed his eyes trying to block out the image of his father leaning over the basket, shouting: 'Bernard! What are you trying to do? Cause an accident and kill us?'

The words had gone round and round Bernard's head as he watched the balloon rise higher and higher, his father's angry face eventually disappearing, his mother's pleas for his father to calm down fading until all he could hear was the sound of the birds crying an almost mocking *ha, ha, ha*.

He'd stood for ten minutes or more watching his parents fly further away, relieved that his feet were firmly on the ground but most of all, that the balloon had righted itself. No harm had been done. He knew his father, quick to forgive and bursting with tales of the sights they had seen from above, would have calmed down by the time they returned and Bernard could explain.

And then, just as he walked back to their Land Rover, he'd heard a gut-wrenching, earth-shuddering explosion and turned to see the balloon in flames. Bernard, not believing what he was seeing, momentarily thought he'd confused the sun with the balloon and glanced around him frantically, squinting into the blinding sun behind him, spooked birds of all shapes and sizes filling the sky.

When he looked back, the balloon was just feet away from crashing along with his whole world.

And worst of all, it'd been all his fault.

Ms Snodgeweed had decided that attending the inquest would be too upsetting for Bernard and had gone instead. She'd called him into her office the next day to tell him the coroner had declared an open verdict. Bernard had asked her what that meant.

'That it was just an unfortunate accident, Bernard.'

'But it wasn't, Miss. It was all my fault. I killed them,' Bernard had sobbed.

'No, Bernard. It was a stupid accident. The gas exploded. Stupid pointless accidents happen all over the world all the time and people die. In fact, I bet that somebody somewhere is probably exploding at this very moment,' Ms Snodgeweed had said, banging the table with her fist to emphasise her point. 'BOOM!'

'But you don't understand. I want to be punished. It was me!'

'Don't be silly, child. You feel guilty because you're alive. Now, in my experience, the more you go on about things, the more upsetting they become. Time to move on,' she'd said as if he'd just had a minor falling out with a friend.

'But - .'

'Shhh! You just have to get on with life. Close the door on your way out,' she'd said, without looking up.

And because Bernard hadn't known what else to do, he did indeed try to get on with life as best as he could. For the first six months he'd been unable to sleep and when he did, he was plagued by nightmares where the accident replayed over again and again, or where his parents appeared with their backs to him, refusing to turn, despite him screaming at them that he was sorry. He was so, so sorry, and that he'd do anything to swap places with them. Because he didn't deserve to be alive.

Like his parents had done to him during their night-time visits, he turned his back on his friends, his studies and food, including Ms Snodgeweed's gifts of exotic sweets from her last minute mercy missions to comfort sick relatives dotted around the world's most desirable holiday destinations.

During the day, he'd bunk off lessons and explore the fields next to the school grounds for hours. On warmer days, he'd sink down in an abandoned bathtub, indulging in dark thoughts and digging his fingers into his temples as if trying to squeeze out all of his badness. And when it rained, he'd climb through the window of a dilapidated summer house where, away from the eyes of the other children, he'd sit and cry until he felt his heart would break.

Yes, he had 'got on with life' as Ms Snodgeweed had advised. But it had been a miserly sliver of a life lived in the shadows cast by normal, unorphanised people. People who hadn't killed their parents.

'Bernard! Bernard!'

Brenda's voice brought Bernard back to the present. He looked up to see the train had already arrived at the station and Brenda was knocking urgently at the window.

'Hurry, Bernard, love. The vet's waiting for you.'

Chapter 23

Sarah-Jane, the vet, pointed across at two giraffes dozing in the morning sun. Right away, Bernard spotted the bald patches on the base of their necks. They were about the size of two medium-sized guinea pigs.

'And they're not the only ones,' she said, as they walked to an enclosure next door where the zebras were fast asleep.

Bernard winced as he saw large clumps of their fur were missing too, leaving stripes of pink and black skin.

As they toured the zoo, they spotted two gorillas had lost swathes of silver fur from their backs and three mandrills had lost their famous yellow beards. But it was the lemurs who'd been hardest hit. Nearly every single one was missing fur, mostly from their tummies and their backs, and they were now standing in the sun's rays trying to keep their newly bald bodies warm.

Bernard was pleased Loki and Armando hadn't come. He suspected that Armando wouldn't mind losing a bit of hair but the vain Loki, whose long thick golden fur attracted much admiration, would be miserable without his.

'What do you think it is?' asked Bernard.

Sarah-Jane sucked in her breath as she peered at the lemurs.

'It could be a case of collective alopecia.'

'Alopeesha? What's that?' asked Bernard.

'Unexplained hair loss. Humans get it too. It can be brought on by stress.'

'Stress? What have they got to be stressed about? They've got brand new enclosures and climbing platforms!' said Brenda.

'Perhaps Bunny's death has affected them more than we thought,' said Sarah-Jane, gravely.

'Though what about the tigers? They loved Bunny the most and they still have all theirs,' Bernard pointed out. 'And the warthogs don't appear to have lost their wiry bristles.'

'True enough,' admitted Sarah-Jane. 'It could be something simple like fleas. They could all be rubbing their fur off when they have a good old itch.'

'There are no fleas at Fluffingdale Zoo,' Bernard said, crossing his arms. 'We de-flea all the animals once a month. And anyway, surely there'd be tell-tale traces of fur on the fences where they'd been scratching their itches,' he added.

'Though it was very windy last night, Bernard. It could have blown away. But fleas or mange don't fit because I can't see any sore patches or scabs,' said Sarah-Jane.

Bernard leaned over the low wooden fence, peering at the patchiest of the lemurs, its bedraggled appearance putting him in mind of the raggedy creature he'd seen earlier that morning lurking in the garden.

'It couldn't be some kind of skin condition brought in from animals outside the zoo, could it?' asked Bernard.

Sarah-Jane and Brenda's eyes widened as Bernard relayed

what he'd seen that morning, all too aware that the two listen-
ers were exchanging nervous glances throughout.

'...and I felt sorry for the creature whatever it was. Its fur
was in a terrible state,' he said, concluding his account.

'I just hope it's not...' Sarah-Jane muttered.

'Not what?' asked Bernard.

Brenda slapped her hand over her mouth before mum-
bling: 'Oh, please no!'

'Well, they are unusually sleepy which is the other main
symptom. Did they play after breakfast?' asked Sarah-Jane.

'No, come to think of it they were all fast asleep when I
arrived and the zookeepers said they barely opened their eyes
at breakfast time. Some of them, like the zebras, didn't even
bother eating breakfast and carried on sleeping,' said Brenda.

'They're usually all waiting at the gates for their food and
then go and play straight afterwards,' said Bernard.

'Oh dear, not again,' said Sarah-Jane, dramatically.

'No! Please, don't!' said Brenda, even more dramatically.

'There have been outbreaks before...all hushed up, of
course,' said Sarah-Jane.

It was now Bernard's turn to throw nervous glances at
Sarah-Jane and then back again at Brenda while the two
women shook their heads slowly, muttering to themselves.

'Will someone please just tell me what's going on?' he demanded.

'You tell him,' said Brenda. 'I can't bring myself to say the
word.'

'What word?' asked Bernard.

'Go on! You're the professional,' said Brenda.

'Oh, if I must,' said Sarah-Jane, pausing for a moment before whispering: 'Fluffititus.'

'Fluffititus?' repeated Bernard loudly.

'Shhhh. Keep your voice down. We don't want to scare people,' scolded Brenda.

'And if it is, we'll have to close the zoo down,' whispered Sarah-Jane.

'What do you mean close the zoo?' asked Bernard, even more confused now.

'He's too young to remember the Great Guinea Pig Massacre,' said Brenda. 'You tell him. It sickens me to talk of it.'

Sarah-Jane hesitated for a moment before taking a deep breath and beginning.

'Well, back in the 1970s, Bernard, Britain was a very different place. For a start we didn't have things like smart phones and the internet, but we did have flared trousers, big hair and a hell of a lot of guinea pigs. In fact, we were swamped by them. A craze that had started in the early 1960s had grown out of control.

'You see, they were very popular as pets but soon they began escaping and breeding in the wild. It got to the point when you couldn't walk down the street without tripping over some double or triple-crowned guinea pig scuttling around. They were taking over, nesting in our walls, our attics, eating through telephone wires, blocking our drains, coming up through toilets, interfering with air traffic control and MI5 communications, jamming machines in factories. You name a disaster, there'd be a guinea pig behind it, or *in* it. Well, the government had to do something. These guinea pigs were bringing the British economy to its knees. So they got some scientists to come up with a virus that would kill them off.'

'Except it didn't just kill guinea pigs. It killed all the animals in the trial zone,' added Brenda.

'And you can guess where that trial zone was, Bernard,' said Sarah-Jane.

'Not Fluffingdale?'

'Afraid so.'

Bernard gasped, thinking of all the poor dead guinea pigs.

'At first, they thought it'd worked,' continued Sarah-Jane. 'The guinea pigs disappeared and the scientists were hailed as heroes, and they planned to introduce the virus to the rest of Britain. But then a few days later, farmers and pet owners noticed that animals were losing patches of fur, here and there, before eventually it all fell out and they'd find them dead as doornails the next day.'

Bernard looked down at a sleeping lemur and stroked what little fur was left on its tummy.

'No, Bernard. No touching,' said Brenda swiping his hand away. 'That's the other thing, you see. It had the opposite effect on humans. Farmers and the protestors who tried to save the guinea pigs started noticing that they were sprouting little patches of guinea pig fur on their hands and sometimes on their faces.'

Bernard tried to take in everything they'd told him while examining his fingers, waiting for little hairs to begin sprouting.

'Come on. Let's get your hands washed,' said Sarah-Jane. 'I'm sorry, Bernard but the last outbreak was 15 years ago and killed a lot of the farm animals and pets around here. We'll have no other option but to close the zoo.'

'But...but...surely it's just a skin disease? Why don't we put some cream on it and see if it goes away. I mean there must be other symptoms with this fluffititus other than losing fur?' asked Bernard.

'Yes, as we've already said, Bernard. Sleepiness,' said Sarah-Jane motioning at the lemur enclosure where all but two were now either fast asleep on the grass, or dozing up against trees.

'But isn't there anything we can do for the animals? There must be a vaccine?' he asked.

'There is but it doesn't work if they've already got the disease. I'm afraid, if it is fluffititus, it's kinder to put them down.'

'But you can't just kill them!' said Bernard, realising his words echoed those he spoke last year when Von Hesti planned to shoot the zoo animals for pleasure.

He thought of all they'd done to make the zoo a success. And for what? For some stupid man-made disease to claim their lives?

'Listen. It may not be fluffititus. I need take some blood samples and get them analysed but we won't know until they come back from the lab,' said Sarah-Jane, trying to reassure Bernard. 'Until then, you need to close the zoo to the public. Keep an eye on them, and if any more fur goes missing, ring me, whatever the time, day or night.'

Chapter 24

The rest of the morning was spent pacifying cross parents and coach drivers, and apologising to disappointed children who'd travelled far and wide to watch Emile, Zola and Titus' performance and visit the zoo animals. Afterwards, Sarah-Jane showed Bernard and the zookeepers how to set up disinfectant zones around each enclosure where they would have to wash down their boots and gloves with special anti-fluffitis liquid after checking on the animals every hour.

By the afternoon, everyone was relieved to see the animals running around as normal. But, most importantly, there were no more missing patches of fur reported.

So, by the time he returned to Fluffingdale Farm late that night, Bernard was feeling positive about the animals' fate. It looked highly likely they were suffering a simple skin complaint after all or, if it were fluffititus, then the virus had weakened because the attack was mild.

However, as soon as he went into the house, his good mood disappeared. A note, penned by Larold, was stuck to the kitchen door. Bernard immediately felt his anger at Larold for poking her nose into his parents' deaths boiling up again.

'What's she been up to now?' said Bernard to the empty hallway as he tore down the note and read it.

Dear Bernard,

I'm sorry I upset you earlier. I've left you some vegan pig chops in the fridge and something on your desk that you might find interesting. Hope the animals are okay.

Night, night.

Lx

'Vegan pig chops?' said Bernard, despairing at Larold's ignorance.

But even if Bernard did want to tuck into the so-called vegan pig chops, he had no appetite. Anything but. Along with all the staff at the zoo, he'd been stuffing himself with sandwiches set to go off while the zoo was closed. And as for what was on his desk, it could wait. Bernard certainly didn't want to do anything Larold had suggested after their quarrel.

He began to climb the stairs to bed. But as he did so, a horrible thought fluttered around his head: what if she's put two and two together and suspects the truth? *That I was responsible for the balloon exploding. That I killed my parents.* He stopped and uncrumpled the note in his hand, his heart rate quickening as he re-read the line: *Something on your desk that you might find interesting.*

He took in a deep breath and breathed out slowly, realising that he was being silly because no-one knew except for him. There hadn't been anyone around as it was so early in the morning. Even the man who owned the hot air balloon had gone back home to bed once he'd helped them to set it up, knowing that Bernard's parents were both experienced pilots. Maybe, just maybe, she was trying to be nice, trying to make up for digging up the past, thought Bernard. Maybe she's just found an article about anteaters?

But dark thoughts bombarded him from every direction until he was so wide awake that he had no other choice but to march downstairs to the office and find out exactly what was waiting for him.

Bernard slumped into his chair, staring at the small red folder with a bright pink post it note on top shouting: 'Read me!'

He grabbed it, opened it up and took out several sheets of paper before glimpsing a headline at the top of one:

Mystery deepens into conservationists' deaths.

'I thought you were my friend,' he said, shoving its contents back inside the folder and throwing it into the fireplace.

Chapter 25

Bernard awoke with a start and blinked back the pale morning light dribbling through the curtains. He stretched his neck, wondering why it was so achy, before realising he wasn't in bed but slumped over his desk.

He sat up and glanced down at a photo of particularly fine anteater strolling through the wetlands of Brazil known as the Pantanal. In the background, a capybara, a giant guinea pig, peeked out shyly through some bushes.

Then memories of the night before came flooding back. His eyes wandered to the fireplace where the folder was splayed over the hearth. He glanced at the clock. It was only 5.45am. He snapped his eyes shut trying to block out thoughts of the folder's contents.

'Why do you have to interfere, Larold?' said Bernard, scooping up the folder and shoving it into a drawer.

After making a cup of tea, Bernard went outside into the garden, marvelling at the birth of the new day as the head of the giant sun crowned over the horizon, its rays wiping away the darkness of night.

Before the fateful ballooning accident, this used to be his favourite time of the day. He loved the quiet and unhurried feeling of early morning. Of course, he knew Ryan would already be milking the cows and, beyond Fluffingdale, people were getting ready for work, while night workers were nearing the end of their shifts at hospitals and care homes.

But it felt as though the world belonged to just him and the birds, and this morning he wished more than anything that it would remain so. Because he knew if he opened the folder, the day would bring him heartache.

It was time to tell Larold the truth about his parents' deaths: that whatever question marks she'd read about in the media were down to him.

'Time to be brave,' said Bernard, feeling anything but.

He drained the last drops of tea and walked back to the office. But as he did so, he caught a flash of fur darting across the field next door. And it was coming straight towards the house.

Bernard watched the same raggedy beast he'd seen the day before hop over the gate into the far corner of the garden, scuttle along the hedge before coming to a sudden stop, as if it'd just noticed his presence. He peered at the creature in the early morning light, trying to work out what exotic species it belonged to.

But he'd never seen anything like it, even in the darkest depths of the Amazon, which harboured all sorts of odd-looking creatures, including insects that look like miniature chickens.

The animal's patchy grey and white fur was alight with little flames of gold matching the sunrise, yet it was quite bald in some places. Perhaps, odder still, were the patches of yellow fur shaped like beards as if it were trying to disguise itself as a marauding gang of blonde-bearded Vikings, cleverly tricking its enemies as to where its head was. It was much taller than he'd remembered and, as he examined its feet sticking out below its strange baggy fur coat, Bernard felt his knees give way.

Because it didn't just have one pair of feet.

Or two pairs.

But three.

'What kind of monstrous freak are you?' cried Bernard, flattening himself against the wall of the house.

Fearing any sudden movement would cause the beast to attack, he slowly edged towards the office door. And as if mimicking his actions, the mysterious creature inched its way along the hedgerow until it reached the plum tree. There it stopped as if, despite being observed and in danger, it was unable to resist plundering several dozen juicy plums.

Bernard fumbled in his pocket for his phone, hoping to snap the beast as its many arms harvested the fruit.

But, instead of stuffing the plums into its many bearded mouths, the creature began hurling the plums at Bernard who threw himself dramatically to the floor. A few of the plum bullets smashed into his body, but, thankfully, the creature's aim was atrocious and most exploded on the ground and against the house.

After the bombardment came to a sudden halt, Bernard peeked up to see the beast galloping across the orchard towards the monkeys' play area. Realising the creature could be suffering from the dreaded fluffititus, Bernard scrambled to his feet. He needed to catch it before it spread the disease to Emile, Titus, Zola, Armando and Loki. Bernard sprinted across the orchard, desperate to stop the beast but found himself flying to the ground as he tripped over a fallen branch. He looked up in time to see the flurry of fur scarpering towards the monkeys' play area.

'No, not near the monkeys, please. Come back here!' he yelled.

He ran up to the gate and leapt over it into the play area, but missed his footing and crashed straight into Emile and Zola who were on his old tyre swing, clinging onto each other, their little bodies shaking in fear.

'Thank God, you're all right,' said Bernard, quickly examining them for any wounds before suddenly realising Titus was missing.

'Don't tell me the beast has snatched him?'

Zola and Emile gestured to the tree house just as Titus appeared on the platform and climbed down to join his brother and sister.

'Thank you!' said Bernard, gazing up at the sky, though he wasn't sure who he was thanking.

'You must have been terrified. You poor things. Did it...did it...try and...attack you?' asked Bernard, imagining its huge jaws gobbling up his precious monkeys. 'Now you need to be brave. I just need to know one thing: which way did it go?'

The monkeys all looked at one another and shook their heads as if they weren't quite sure what Bernard was talking about.

'Towards Fluffingdale or the farm?' pointed Bernard in both directions.

Titus pointed to the farm, while Emile and Zola pointed towards Fluffingdale. Seeing which way his brother and sister were pointing, Titus quickly changed his mind and copied them.

'Mmm,' said Bernard, knowing that Titus wasn't the most observant of the monkeys. 'Come on. Let's get back to the house. It'll be safer there,' he added, scanning the fields for any sign of the beast.

Thankfully, there was none. So, he picked up the monkeys and hurried back to the house, all the while stroking their backs to calm them, noticing how their skin was sticky with sweat, praying it was caused by fear, not by the dreaded fluffititus. He couldn't bear to lose Emile, Zola and Titus.

He rushed into the kitchen to find the first aid box, took their temperatures and watched them gulp down three spoonfuls of anti-fever medicine each, while he gulped back the urge to cry.

Chapter 26

'So much for their raging fevers,' said Larold as the monkeys ran off to their rooms giggling.

'It does look a bit…a bit…' stuttered Bernard, trying to find the right words for her artist's impression of the mystery beast.

Larold had offered to capture the creature's likeness from Bernard's description so they would have something to show to the police. Something he now regretted agreeing to as he glanced at Larold's thunderous face.

'A bit what? Bernard. Spit it out.'

'Er…a little bit…mad?'

'Yes, and that's the description you and the monkeys gave to me.'

'It didn't really look like a caterpillar, to be honest,' said Bernard, trying not to laugh at the deranged-looking creature picking plums.

'But you said it had loads of feet and hands.'

'Six possibly. Not hundreds.'

'Well, I'm terribly sorry, Mr…Plumhead,' said Larold, scrunching up the picture and throwing it at Bernard.

'No need to be like that,' said Bernard, ducking and then flinching as the door slammed in reply.

He slumped into his chair and began picking out the bits

of mashed plum from his hair, contemplating his life at the moment. If it wasn't the monkeys messing around, it was Larold complaining about their behaviour. He couldn't win.

And now he had an even bigger worry to deal with - the monkeys being infected with fluffititus after their run in with the mystery beast.

As he removed a drying glob of plum from his fringe, he glimpsed the blue cardboard folder Larold had left for him the night before and felt his heart sink even further. It was sticking out of his drawers like a tongue as if it to say, 'Stop ignoring me!'

Bernard put his mushy plum-covered head in his hands. His confession would have to wait.

***

Just to be safe, he sent Armando and Loki to live with Brenda and watched over Emile, Zola and Titus like a hawk, constantly checking their temperatures and looking for any signs of fur loss.

Although the monkeys' breathing and temperatures returned to normal soon after their shock encounter with the beast, Bernard couldn't stop fretting.

When he went to check on them every morning, they were extremely drowsy like the zoo animals, and Bernard was convinced that it was only a matter of time before fluffititus finished them off.

To make matters worse, his nights were full of lurid nightmares where he woke to find Titus's and Emile's much-loved quiffs on their pillows and Zola's ginger Mohican lying on her sheets as the disease ravaged their little bodies.

Back at the zoo, more and more animals were losing their

fur. Now all but five lemurs, one giraffe, one zebra and one mandrill were completely bald and the gorillas had lost all their precious silver fur from their backs. Brenda's knitting group had worked night and day to provide warm clothes for many of the creatures, but the jumpers, tank tops, scarves and hats were no substitute for their natural coats and the animals looked piteous and dejected without their fur.

Bernard was about to call Sarah-Jane, the vet, to give her an update on the fifth night's fur loss, when she came running into the zoo office, followed by Ryan.

'Negative! Negative! Negative!' she chanted as they danced around in celebration.

But, however delighted they were that the threat of fluffititus would no longer darken the valleys of Fluffingdale, and all the animals could breathe a big collective sigh of relief, the problem of the missing fur remained.

Once they'd stopped conga-ering around the room, Bernard asked the inevitable: 'If it's not fluffititus, what is it?'

'Well, this may have something to do with it,' said Sarah-Jane, fishing out a tall old-fashioned green glass bottle from her giant vet's bag.

'We found it discarded in the bushes by the entrance,' explained Ryan. 'I thought it was rubbish chucked away by one of your littering visitors but as I was putting it in the recycling bin, I noticed this,' he added, pointing to the label.

Unintelligible oriental script danced in front of their eyes. Bernard and Brenda looked at one another and shrugged.

Registering their bewildered looks, Ryan quickly twisted the bottle round to show the other side of the label which was in English and read: *Dr Wu's Sleepy-Sleepy Now Infusion. Fed up with annoying visitors or pets? This efficient, tasteless sleeping potion will keep them quiet for up to 16 hours at a time! Two drops in cup of tea or any beverage induces sleep.*

Directly beneath the label were printed several testimonials from happy customers.

'Dr Wu's Sleepy-Sleepy Now Infusion is a miracle! Our neighbours no longer bother us with their early morning DIY! Thank you, Dr Wu!' Ms M Verity, Folkestone, UK.

'A perfect Xmas with very quiet relatives!' Ms J Sutton, Sydney, Australia.

'I didn't think these kind of medicines were legal,' said Brenda.

'If it's got anything to do with Dr Wu then I doubt any of them are,' said Bernard.

'No, none of these ingredients are legal,' confirmed Sarah-Jane, studying the label closely. 'In fact, I'd say all of them are highly illegal. And who is this Dr Wu, anyway, Bernard?'

'Let's just say she was keen on getting hold of the hairless monkeys for some of her so-called quack medicines,' answered Bernard, suddenly wondering whether Sebastian, Virgil and her were up to their old tricks again, but this time using the animals' hair.

But he couldn't imagine how or why. Sebastian was a now recluse in Barbados with Virgil. Surely he wouldn't risk breaking his deal with Larold? And what would he be doing with a mixture of hair unless he wanted to weave matching multi-furred wigs to cover his and Boghero's bald heads?

They walked over to the lemur enclosure, watching the creatures' little tummies rising and falling in a deep sleep.

'Well, whoever used this medicine is obviously drugging

the animals and then taking their fur,' said Sarah-Jane, examining a snoring lemur. 'And by state of their fur or rather lack of it, I'd say they were probably being shaved.'

'Shaved?' echoed Bernard.

'But why would anyone do that?' asked Brenda.

'I don't know. Maybe some weirdo who likes to take their fur, maybe as trophies?' offered Sarah-Jane. 'Bernard, who else knows about Dr Wu apart from you?'

'Er…Larold. But why would she want their fur?' laughed Bernard.

Brenda, Ryan and Sarah-Jane glanced at one another and then at Bernard.

'You've not known her very long, have you?' said Brenda. 'And she is related to that Sebastian. Maybe there's bad blood running through her veins too,' she added, reaching down into her handbag.

Bernard half-expected her to pull out a police file marked LAROLD THE PHANTOM FUR THIEF in giant capital letters, or at the very least, a giant finger of suspicion and point it towards Fluffingdale Farm where his friend was looking after the monkeys.

Instead, she pulled out a bag of mints and offered them around. As Bernard sucked on his, he tried to see Larold in a whole new light. Perhaps, Brenda was right. He didn't know the first thing about her. He went over their conversation when he'd first spotted the mystery creature in the garden. Hadn't she mentioned shaving and shaven sheep? But what possible reason would she have for stealing fur? It didn't make any sense.

'Has she ever shown any obvious interest in the animal's fur? Loki, for example?' asked Sarah-Jane.

'No!' said Bernard. 'No more than anyone else when in the company of a super-furred cat.'

'She loves them tigers,' said Brenda, suspiciously.

'Oh, hang on a moment,' said Bernard, feeling disloyal. 'You can't go around accusing...'

'It's all a bit of coincidence that Mr Stripey and Marley are the only ones not to have lost any of their fur,' interrupted Brenda.

'Not really considering their man-eating reputation,' said Bernard. 'Anyway, what about that patchy beast thing that plummed me this morning? I'd say it was suffering the same illness as our animals. It was very strange. In fact, I'd say I've never seen anything like it...I swear it had three pairs of legs and arms. They moved like lightning.'

'I checked with the local police and there's been no other reports of any strange creatures in the area,' said Sarah-Jane.

'And I've checked with all the other farms and there's not been one report of any strange animals,' said Ryan.

'It seems you're the only one to have seen it. Perhaps the stress of everything has made you see things,' said Brenda, ruffling his hair before taking it away swiftly and declaring: 'Eugh! You've got some kind of soft fruit in your hair.'

'Yes, I told -,' said Bernard before being interrupted.

'Probably just an escaped sheep with mange,' said Sarah-Jane dismissively. 'It's rife at the moment.'

'Right! Next time, I'll make sure I get a photo of it,' said Bernard, feeling cross that no-one was taking his sighting seriously despite the cast iron evidence of plum in his hair.

He certainly knew what a sheep with mange looked like and it had absolutely no resemblance to the beast he'd seen in the garden.

They stood for a few moments sucking on their mints as if the flavour held magical mystery solving properties.

Ryan, who had been very quiet up to this point, crunched on his mint loudly and then spoke. 'The only other suspects I can think of...' he hesitated as he swallowed the mint down. 'And I know you won't like this, Bernard...'

'Yes,' they said, collectively.

'Those monkeys of yours.'

'What?' said Bernard. 'That's ridiculous! First you accuse Larold and now -'

'Just hear him out, Bernard,' said Brenda, laying a hand on Bernard's arm.

'They are fond of pulling Bob's fur out at times. And if you don't mind me saying, it's exactly the kind of spiteful thing they'd do.'

'Oh, come on. How on earth would they get here? Let alone order *Dr Wu's Sleepy-Sleepy Now Potion*?' protested Bernard, bristling at the suggestion that his monkeys were spiteful.

He looked at Sarah-Jane and Brenda for support, expecting them to laugh off the fantastical theory but they continued sucking on their mints, nodding their heads as if they were seriously considering Ryan's accusation.

Then Brenda spoke. 'I'm not sure how they get here, Bernard,' she said, 'but as far as ordering things on the internet is concerned, we all know they're very capable of doing that, don't we? Remember the big credit card bill they ran up on them computer games?'

'But...but...that was just games,' stuttered Bernard. 'This is just...silly. First and foremost they have no motive.'

'Oh, and what about that shipping container full of gigantic bananas from Costa Rica that turned up out of the blue two years ago,' said Brenda. 'And then there was the lorry load of fermented asparagus. It absolutely stank the village out for days.'

'Oh, yes. Even Carol's pigs were thinking of upping sticks. Revolting it was,' laughed Ryan. 'But not quite as revolting as those sparkly designer shellsuits. Remember them?' added Ryan, rolling his eyes.

'I do indeed,' exclaimed Brenda. '£5,000 worth!'

'That was a simple mistake -' spluttered Bernard.

'Open your eyes, Bernard, love,' said Brenda. 'Have you forgot about your poor teddies already? Bear, Tiger and Panda gutted, skinned and turned into handbags and rugs.'

Sarah-Jane gasped. 'Never!'

'That was ages ago -'

'I'd say the bald truth, no pun intended, is them being partially hairless is a pretty big motive,' said Ryan.

'True enough,' said Sarah-Jane.

'Mmm, time to see the truth, my love,' said Brenda nodding her head in agreement and popping another mint into her mouth.

'Right! This has gone far enough. As the owner of Fluffingdale Zoo, I am officially discounting that theory for being too silly,' said Bernard, suddenly feeling as if everyone in the room was picking on him and his monkeys.

'Bernard, love, we're just trying to solve the mystery of the missing fur. There's no need to get all uppity,' said Brenda, placing an arm around Bernard's shoulders.

'I'm telling you they would not do this! It's an outrageous accusation,' said Bernard.

'Now, now,' said Ryan. 'You know them better than anyone else so we'll respect your wishes and talk no more of it.'

'Good!' said Bernard.

'Which leaves just one suspect,' said Ryan. 'Larold. We need you to keep a close eye on her and see if you can find anything out.'

'Really?' said Bernard.

'I think it would be wise,' said Sarah-Jane. 'Just so we can rule her out.'

'Another mint, anyone?' asked Brenda.

Chapter 27

During the train journey home that evening Bernard felt himself bristle as he recalled what Ryan had said about the monkeys.

Spiteful.

It wasn't a word he'd ever associate with Emile, Zola and Titus. Naughty and mischievous maybe. But they were never nasty.

Bernard realised that Ryan had never forgiven the monkeys reaction to Bob when they first arrived, wanting to ride on his back. But they'd been just babies. Of course, they wanted to play with Bob. And okay, their fingers may have got caught up in his fur but they hadn't meant to pull it, let alone pull it out.

As for Brenda accusing Larold of having so-called bad blood, it was pure nonsense. Larold didn't have single drop of bad blood in her, he was sure of it. Sebastian had taken it all for himself.

And anyway, she'd been the one who'd alerted him to Sebastian's evil plan. Hadn't she saved Emile, Zola and Titus from being crunched into Dr Wu's quack miracle hair restorer?

But perhaps, he suddenly realised, she'd only saved the

monkeys to gain his trust and get easy access to the zoo animals? No, thought, Bernard. It was as ridiculous a theory as blaming the monkeys. What possible motive would she have for stealing the fur? Absolutely none.

So, as he got off the train and walked home, enjoying the warm evening air, he resolved he would never ever cast the teeniest-tiniest slither of suspicion over Larold. He hatched a plan where he'd pretend to Ryan, Brenda and Sarah-Jane that he was doing as they requested, watching her closely. Then he'd report nothing back because there would be a big fat nothing to report.

'I'm home,' he called, walking through the front door. His voice echoed down the corridor and moments later, Emile, Zola and Titus came scuttling along the hallway.

'That's a welcome and a half,' he said, bending down to greet the monkeys.

But instead of gently jumping up to say hello, they nearly knocked him off his feet as they swerved around him and hid behind his legs.

'You haven't been fighting Armando and Loki again?' said Bernard, steeling himself for having to sort out yet another upset between the two parties.

Then he realised they couldn't have been because Armando and Loki were still at Brenda's who'd arranged to bring them home after work tomorrow now the fluffititus scare was over.

'What is it? What's wrong?'

Bernard's heart began to race as he suddenly wondered if the raggedy beast had managed to break into the house.

A moment later, the answer arrived in the form of Larold's

voice booming down the corridor, followed by her heavy foot-steps.

'I'LL TEACH YOU A LESSON,' she shouted.

The monkeys scampered onto Bernard's back and he stepped onto the staircase out of sight.

Perhaps Brenda had been right to be suspicious of Larold after all.

'COME BACK HERE,' she shouted as she reached the staircase. 'You'll regret the day you mess with me!'

'Oh really?' said Bernard, peering down at her from the step.

'AHHHH!' screamed Larold. 'Oh, Bernard, you gave me a fright...' she said, holding onto her heart before noticing the monkeys' hiding place.

'There you are,' she said, grabbing at the monkeys' legs.

'Stop it, Larold. What have you done to them? They're absolutely terrified of you,' said Bernard as the monkeys whimpered in his ears.

'What have *I* done to them? You mean what have *they* done to me?' said Larold, swiping at Emile's quiff.

'Leave them alone!'

'I will not! They've been up in my room messing with my things.'

'I'm sure they're just playing,' said Bernard, trying to peel the monkey's fingers away from his neck. 'Weren't you?'

The monkeys nodded but still refused to get down.

'Bernard, you're such a soft touch. Come and see if you don't believe me.'

'I am *not* a soft touch. And there's no need for all this shouting and gallivanting around the house.'

'Oh, isn't there?' Larold said, marching up the stairs. 'I'd like to see what you'd do if they'd been messing with your special things.'

Bernard followed. He tried to keep his balance as the monkeys desperately hung onto him with their legs and tried to grip the staircase bannister with their tails and arms, in a bid to stop him from following.

'I did tell you to always lock your room,' said Bernard, trying to unpeel the monkeys' limbs from the banister.

'Er...I did. They obviously got the key and opened it. See!' said Larold as she flung open her door.

Bernard felt his jaw drop as he took in the state of the room. It looked as if...well, a gang of monkeys had broken in because well, that's what actually happened. Bookshelves and chest of drawers had been knocked over spilling ornaments, clothes and books everywhere. The curtains were hanging off the rails, the sheets had been ripped off the bed and lay scattered around the room and Larold's shampoo and bath lotions had been emptied all over the bathroom and bedroom floors.

As he surveyed the devastation, Bernard's eye was drawn to a metal box lying upside down near the bed.

'Look at it. They have no respect. And after all I did for them!' shouted Larold, following Bernard's eye.

She scuttled over to the box, picked it up and slammed it shut but not before Bernard had glimpsed something very interesting inside it: a sizeable clump of light brown hair – suspiciously similar to the fur once belonging to the two incredibly rare dancing lemurs.

'And all because I told them off for teasing Bob,' she said.

'Bob?' said Bernard absent-mindedly as a memory came back to him. How Larold had taken to Loki and Armando, but had never gotten on with the monkeys since coming to live with him. She'd told him a few times that she thought them spoilt. But perhaps, it was more than that. Perhaps she had some weird fur fetish and the real reason she despised them was because they weren't very hairy.

'Ryan dropped by with some milk,' said Larold, clutching the box behind her back, 'and before we knew it, they'd jumped in the back of the Land Rover and they were trying to pull clumps of his fur out. Poor Bob.'

'Well, he must have done something to scare them. Sheep-dogs are always barky, especially Bob. Perhaps he snapped at them,' he said, wondering if he should just make a grab for the box and unmask the phantom fur shaver here and now.

'Only after they attacked him first. He was just sitting in the Land Rover, minding his own business,' she said, moving over to her now righted bedside cabinet and placing the box inside. 'Are you going to tell them off then?' she added, angrily.

'I was just about to,' said Bernard, turning to the monkeys. 'Emile, Zola and Titus. I didn't bring you up to behave like this. What have you got to say for yourselves?' he said, unpeeling their fingers and dropping them to the floor.

The monkeys clung onto one another and stuck out their bottom lips, looking up at him and then at Larold. They then ambled over to Larold and hugged her legs.

'Ok, ok, you can get off now...' she said, pushing them away.

'Tomorrow you apologise to Bob but for now you can

start clearing up,' demanded Bernard, who realised the time had passed to confront her about the box's contents.

He would have to sneak back later to investigate. Then he could take a sample and meet Sarah-Jane at the zoo to compare it to what little fur was left on the dancing lemurs. If there was a match, well, then...he would have to cross that bridge when it came to it.

Bernard watched Larold patiently folding the items of clothes the monkeys were picking up from the floor. Was she really the phantom fur shaver? Had she fooled them all?

Bernard turned away quickly as he felt tears prickling at the thought that his new friend was perhaps not who she seemed to be after all.

Chapter 28

After the monkeys had helped clear up the mess they made, Bernard sent them straight to bed without any warm coconut milk as a punishment. He then went downstairs to check on Larold and was pleased to see *Bouffant Bay*, her favourite soap opera, had just started. He yawned exaggeratedly, wished Larold a goodnight and fetched a torch from the downstairs cupboard before jogging upstairs and sneaking into her room.

The metal box was key to finding out the truth, although Bernard realised if Larold was harvesting all the fur, for whatever bizarre reason, then she'd need a far larger storage container to keep it in. He began by searching her bedside cabinet where he'd seen her hide the box. But there was no sign of it. He then rummaged through a large chest of drawers, feeling increasingly guilty for rifling through all her private possessions and clothes.

However, he could find no evidence. Not even a single human hair, let alone a zoo-full of fur. After searching her wardrobe, he shone the torch around the room, hoping the hiding place would suddenly reveal itself. Instead, the beam caught the edge of the bedspread. It had been thrown messily over the bed covering what lay beneath.

'Obvious hiding place number one,' he whispered.

Bernard dived under the bed but misjudged the distance and crashed headfirst into one of its legs, knocking the bedspread over him and the torch out of his hand.

To an outside observer, it looked as though the bedspread was his mortal enemy as he thrashed around wildly, trying to free himself. And the more he thrashed around, the more entangled he became until it felt as though he was swaddled like a baby. Bernard, realising he had lost the battle against the bedspread, as well as his sense of direction, decided he had no other option but to turn onto his tummy and wriggle along like a caterpillar until he found the door.

But straight away...

BASH!

He knocked into a solid piece of furniture, a chest of drawers or bedside table, he guessed, and several objects rained down on him before crashing to the floor. Bernard began to panic as he realised his secret mission to Larold's bedroom was turning into a disaster. She'd have to be deaf not to hear the loud thuds on the floorboards and he began desperately wriggling in another direction until...

BASH!

His head a wall. Footsteps pounded up the stairs and Bernard quickly wormed his way backwards towards what he hoped was the bed, all the while the footsteps on the stairs getting louder and louder.

'Emile, Zola and Titus, I'm going to kill you,' growled Larold from the other side of the closed door.

Bernard stifled a groan as he hit his head again against the side of something hard just as she burst into the room. He froze as he heard the squeak of a footstep on a floorboard.

'Hang on a moment. Unless you've formed yourself into a human shape, Emile, Titus and Zola, I'd say this looks suspiciously like a Bernard shape,' said Larold, prodding Bernard with her foot before asking: 'Why are you on the floor of my bedroom rolled up in my bedspread?'

'Oh, hi,' said Bernard, trying to sound as if being wrapped up in Larold's bedspread on the floor of her bedroom was the most natural place for him to be in the world.

'Are you stuck?'

'Er...' considered Bernard. 'I think I might be.'

'I should leave you like that,' said Larold crossly. 'As a punishment for sneaking into my room.'

'Please don't,' squeaked Bernard, who was feeling rather light-headed after all the bangs to his head, not to mention the lack of oxygen.

Larold tugged at the side of the bedspread several times before Bernard emerged from the tomb, hot, sweaty and a little breathless.

'Zola said she'd lost her bunny and I thought ...' he said, avoiding eye contact. 'She may have left it here.'

'Oh, really?' said Larold, sounding very unconvinced.

'Yes. She woke up and asked me to come and find it.'

'Which rabbit?'

'The pink one.'

'The one she gutted two days ago?'

'Er, it's a new one.'

Larold sighed. 'So you weren't looking for this then?' she asked, holding out the metal box in her hands.

'What? A box? No. Why should I...' he stammered.

'Please stop lying, Bernard,' she interrupted. 'I saw you eyeing it up earlier and realised what you must have been thinking.'

'No, not all, Larold. You must be imagining it.'

'Bernard, you are a rubbish liar.'

Bernard sank back down on the floor exhausted by his fight with the bedspread. 'Am I really that bad?'

'The worst.'

Bernard groaned and told her about the mystery bottle of *Dr Wu's Sleepy-Sleepy Now* infusion discarded at the zoo and how they'd been trying to work out who was stealing the fur and how Brenda suggested it may have been her.

'That's crazy! What would I want with their fur? And you all assumed, because I was the only other person to know about Dr Wu, it must be me?'

'Yes, I mean, no. I didn't believe it for one minute, that's until I saw the fur in your box. What is it?'

Larold sat crosslegged on the floor next to him and sighed. She opened up the box and took out the hair, coiling it around her fingers and stroking it.

'It's the only bit of her I have left,' she said.

Bernard could now see it was obviously human hair, silky brown with a hint of a curl.

'Your mum's hair?'

Larold nodded sadly.

'A few months after she left, just a couple of days after my tenth birthday, I received a special delivery early one morning,' explained Larold. 'I guess she must have timed its delivery as Dad never bothered to get up before 2pm. When I opened it up, there was a key inside with an address. It turned out to be a deposit box in Bond Street. I went straight there and the only thing inside was this note.'

Larold passed him what look like a piece of ancient parchment, handled and reread a thousand times. He read the neat slanting writing.

My darling Larold,

I want you to know that I love you very much and when I'm settled, I WILL come and get you.

PS: Keep this key save and await further instructions.

'And I'm still waiting,' she sniffed, swiping at her tears angrily with the sleeves of her jumper.

Bernard glanced at Larold, thinking how bad things must have been between Larold's parents for her mother to leave her like that. He wasn't sure what to say, so tentatively patted her on her back.

'Anyway, I can't believe you thought I may be stealing the fur. I mean Dr Wu has her own website. There must be thousands of people who know who she is and someone far closer to us than you think.'

'What? You're saying it's Sebastian?'

'No!'

'Virgil Boghero?'

'No!'

'Well, who then?' asked Bernard, looking extremely confused as to who the other suspects could possibly be.

'Oh, Bernard. When will you see what they're really like.'

'Who?'

'Emile, Zola and Titus.'

Bernard stood up.

'Oh, not this nonsense again. Ryan has already accused them and we've all agreed not to go down that road.'

'What do you mean? You've all agreed.'

'Brenda, Sarah-Jane and Ryan. We've all agreed it's a stupid theory.'

'Well, I don't think it is and Ryan obviously doesn't either,' said Larold, now standing, hands on hips.

'It's not in their nature, Larold.'

'Oh, no, of course not. They'd never pull Bob's fur out, trash my room and stick Loki to the kitchen wall, place toilet rolls and hoover tubes over Armando's nose and all the other zillions of bad things they've done that you turn a blind eye to. I tell you what, Bernard. If you trust them so much, then we'll stay up and see what they really get up to at night,' said Larold.

'Okay, I admit, it looks bad when you put it like that but...,' said Bernard, 'you have to believe me, it's not them...they're not capable of doing anything like that. They have far better things to do than sneak around drugging zoo animals and then shaving them.' Bernard paused for a moment before adding: 'Next thing I know you'll be blaming them for...for... global warming.'

'Wouldn't put it past them...You know what I'm going to do?' said Larold, placing her mother's hair back in the box carefully and standing.

'No, and I'm not interested,' said Bernard, sulkily.

'Well, I'm going to tell you even if you're not interested. I'm going to follow their every movement from now on. Even at night-time, I'll be watching them and I'll prove you wrong.'

'Well, I wish you luck because it will be very boring.

They'll be fast asleep in their beds as they have been every night since the fur has gone missing. They can't be in two places at once, can they?'

'But how do you know they were in their rooms all night?' said Larold, pacing the room.

'I just know.'

'Just knowing wouldn't stand up in a police investigation. Just knowing is not an alibi.'

'Well, I say good night to them and look in on them before I go to bed....'

'So you go to bed at 10pm and what time do you wake them up?' asked Larold, coming to a halt in front of Bernard.

'About 8am. 8.30am.'

'And in between say 10pm and 8am do you ever, Bernard Bamuel, visit their room?'

'What is this? A police investigation?' exclaimed Bernard, throwing the bedspread back onto the bed.

'Just answer the question, Bernard. Between the hours of 10pm and 8am do you ever visit their room?'

'Well, no...'

'Exactly. They have no albi.'

Bernard glared at Larold, wondering if this was what it was like to have a brother or sister. One moment you wanted to comfort them, and the next you wanted to kill them.

'Just because you're upset, don't take it out on the monkeys,' said Bernard.

'I'm not taking anything out on them, Bernard. But you need to see what they're really like.'

'Er, excuse me! I know them better than anyone else,' said Bernard, beginning to lose his temper. 'And anyway, if you're so sure of their guilt, how are you going to get the evidence? Sleep outside their room?'

'If I have to.'

'You've got this completely wrong, Larold. They have no motive.'

'Ha! What about jealousy? They hardly have any hair, Bernard. You hang around all day with an overfluffed ginger cat and a hairy anteater and a zoo full of furry animals. How do you think that makes them feel?'

Bernard stared out of the window into the dusky summer light as he considered Larold's words. He'd never seen their partial hairlessness as being a problem. They were just different. But maybe they'd hated being different. And of all people, he should have been aware of how that had made them feel. After all, he'd spent the last few years aching to be normal like other unorphanised people who hadn't been responsible for their parents' deaths.

'Are you all right, Bernard?' asked Larold.

Bernard nodded. It made him feel sad to think they'd possibly been driven to shaving fur from other animals to make up for their lack of their own.

'But what about the beast in the garden who attacked me? Why doesn't anyone take what I saw seriously?'

'Maybe because we already know who the beast is, Bernard,' said Larold, glancing at a framed photo of the monkeys, posing in their trademark sequin leotards.

'What? No way!' Bernard protested. 'They can't possibly be the beast. I mean, they would never attack me like that with the plums,' said Bernard, pushing away the memory of the day the monkeys splashed him while driving past in the chauffeur-driven car.

Larold rolled her eyes.

'You're never going to believe me or anyone until you see it with your own eyes. I'm going to stand guard outside their room all night and you can join me.'

'No,' said Bernard, his eyes widening as a brainwave hit him. 'If we're going to stay up all night, I have a far better plan to catch the fur thief and prove you all wrong.'

Chapter 29

'Torches?'

'Check,' said Bernard, his hand rummaging around in the rucksack.

'Sandwiches, tea and biscuits?'

'Check.'

'Chopped fruit?'

'Check.'

'Walkie-talkies?'

'Check.'

'Sleeping bags?'

'Check.'

'Night vision binoculars?'

'Check.'

'I think that's it,' said Larold.

'Hang on a moment,' said Bernard as he trotted off down the corridor.

'You're not taking anteater books to read, are you?' she complained, following him into the library.

Larold watched him reach up to a bookshelf, his hand searching between two dusty books about anteaters, before pulling out a dull golden key. He then moved a chair in front of the giant portrait of his grandfather hanging over the fire-place.

'Can't quite reach without it,' said Bernard, clambering onto the chair.

He pushed the portrait aside to reveal a safe with a large round handle. Bernard punched in a code and the safe door swung open.

'This will come in handy just in case,' he said, taking out an object wrapped up in an old t-shirt. Bernard opened it up.

'A gun?' asked Larold, stepping back.

'A tranquilliser gun. It belonged to my parents if they had to treat an injured animal,' he explained, placing it into the backpack. 'And,' he added, his hand dipping back into the safe and pulling out what looked like a cheap black plastic bracelet. 'This.'

'What is it?' asked Larold.

'It's a tracker. My parents were carrying out experiments to track elephants and rhinos so that they could catch poach-ers. Look,' he said, pressing a little button on the side of the bracelet. 'It's on now,' he added, rushing to his desk and turn-ing on his laptop before clicking onto a website.

A map of the UK came into view with a little pulsing red dot racing to the south coast until it came to a stop at Folke-stone before zooming into the village of Fluffingdale.

'Er...why don't we put it on one of the monkeys? Then we won't have to go to the zoo. We can just watch from here.'

'Ha, ha. I don't think so, Larold. Because of this one sim-ple fact: the monkeys are innocent. Now I thought I could tackle the culprit to the ground and you could slip it onto them and, at least then, we'll be able to follow them to their lair and find out exactly who they are.'

Larold pulled a face. 'I hardly think whoever is shaving the fur is going to stop halfway through and hold its paw up to me and say, 'There you go, just slip it on.' And anyway, even if I do manage to wrestle it on, won't they just tear it off?'

Bernard tutted. 'There's no need to be so negative, Larold.'

He pushed past her and heaved the rucksack onto his back. 'And we won't ever know if we miss the train. Come on!'

'You're the boss,' sighed Larold.

It was nearly 10.30pm when they set off across the fields to the station, the summer sky only just darkening. An owl kept hooting every few minutes as if it knew what they were up to and wanted everyone else to know too. Bernard found himself edging closer to Larold as the summer light seeped away and found some comfort in realising Larold was doing exactly the same.

'So, what's the plan when we get there?' asked Larold.

'We'll lie in wait on Lemur Island. There are four or five left with a sprinkling of hair and they're a soft target for whoever is stealing the fur.'

Larold nodded.

'There's a large oak tree with a kind of tree house and a large platform where they like to sleep on warm nights. Luckily for us, there's a huge bough above it where we can hide out of sight. We can take it in turns to get some sleep.'

'Bernard.'

'Yes?'

'The thing is I don't really like the dark very much,' whispered Larold.

'It will be fine,' said Bernard, turning on the torch now dusk had turned to night. Though the relief he felt when they arrived at the brightly lit station told a very different story.

Apart from a couple of sleeping commuters, they were the only passengers on the train. As soon as they sat down, Bernard took out a piece of paper from his bag and quickly drew a map of Lemur Island, pointing out key areas such as entrance and exit points. When they arrived at the zoo station, they were the only passengers to alight.

'Whoever's taking the fur certainly isn't getting the last train here,' said Bernard, glancing up and down the deserted platform.

'Unless they're already at the zoo,' suggested Larold.

'They wouldn't risk it – the zookeepers do their last rounds at 10.30pm.'

'But couldn't they have hidden somewhere?'

'Possible but too risky, I'd think. The zookeepers are being extra vigilant.'

Once at the zoo, Bernard and Larold headed straight to Lemur Island to the platform where dozens of bald lemurs, some in sagging jumpers and tank tops, were snuggling up to each other to keep warm.

Larold scattered the cut up fruit to distract them, then they climbed the tree, making a nest in the bough with their sleeping bags.

'It's a bit darker than I thought it would be,' said Larold. 'What's the time?'

'11.11pm. We've only been here five minutes,' said Bernard.

'Really? It seems like hours.'

'Not really.'

Larold sighed. 'This stake out business is nothing like the films, is it?' she said.

'We have an unknown beast to wrestle to the ground. I think that's pretty exciting.'

'Mmm. If it is a beast.'

'Well, I'm sure if we wait long enough I will be proved right,' said Bernard, trying hard to keep the impatience out of his voice.

'Or wrong.'

'Right.'

'Wrong.'

'But if I agree with you, Bernard, then we'll both be wrong,' yawned Larold.

'What?' said Bernard, trying to work out what Larold was saying before snapping. 'No, if *I* agree with *you* we will both be wrong.'

'Whatever.'

After a few moments of sulky silence, Larold whispered: 'It's a bit boring.'

'Well, I'm sorry it's not entertaining enough for you. You can always go and stay at the keeper's cottage.'

'No, it's okay. I wouldn't miss it for the world,' said Larold, getting the flask out and pouring a cup of tea while Bernard surveyed the scene with his night vision binoculars.

'Anything?'

'No, just lots of lemurs sitting around,' he said, trailing the binoculars onto the wooden platform below.

'Nothing new there then,' said Larold. 'It's as if lemurs have been told by whoever invented them to sit and wait for further instructions or they're waiting for a meeting to start or something. Maybe a meeting with aliens who need their help to take over the world.'

'They picked the wrong animals to help then,' said Bernard.

'What do you mean?'

'Lemurs are hardly ruthless power-crazy dictators and, anyway, there's hardly any left in the world. Practically been hunted to extinction.'

'For their fur?'

'No, their meat. They've nowhere to hide because their rainforests has been chopped down.'

'Maybe that's why they hang around all day, waiting for them to grow back again,' pondered Larold before adding: 'I sometimes feel like a lemur. Waiting for Mum to come back.'

'Oh right,' swallowed Bernard. 'It must be hard knowing she's out there somewhere. You know... you can talk to me about her if you want to.'

'Mmm.. I don't like talking about it...because if I do then I may ruin it and then she'll never come back. Is that the same with you?'

'What do you mean?' asked Bernard, suddenly taking up his binoculars again. 'They're never going to come back. My parents are dead.'

'No, I mean, you don't want to think too much about how your parents died. It brings it all back.'

Bernard shrugged. He'd managed to block out what Larold had said about question marks over his parents' deaths for the last two days thanks to all the shenanigans at the zoo.

But now he felt the fear of being exposed as a murderer clawing at the pit of his tummy.

'Bernard, are you ever going to read those reports I printed out?'

'Yes, of course,' he snapped, putting down his binoculars. 'But for now I need to get some sleep,' he added, turning his back on Larold and snuggling down in his sleeping bag. 'Wake me up in an hour's time.'

But Bernard didn't get much sleep. Every time he was about to nod off, his parents' loomed large in his mind and, when he did manage to sleep, he dreamt he was a little boy again, begging them to turn round to look at him. He was about to drift off again when he felt a sharp digging in his side.

'Bernard!' whispered Larold urgently.

'What?' he said sitting bolt upright. 'What's happening? Is the beast - ?'

'I need to go for a wee.'

He looked at his watch. It had only just gone midnight. 'You could have gone before.'

'Tea's gone straight through me,' she said.

'Well, if whoever comes now...'

'What do you want me to do? Wee all over the lemurs? I *need* to go,' interrupted Larold. 'Come on.'

'What do you mean, *come on*?'

'I'm scared of the dark. You'll have to come.'

'I can't leave our post! You'll have to go by yourself.'

'Please.'

'No, it'll be fine. Just go in the bushes. I'll follow your path with the torch beam and you can take a torch with you.'

'Eugh, I don't want you looking at me when I'm going to the toilet.'

'I didn't mean it like that. As soon as you get there, I'll look away.'

'Thanks for nothing,' said Larold as she started climbing down the tree.

Bernard heard a thud and a high-pitched squeal as she landed.

'Sorry! Sorry!' apologised Larold.

'Be careful!' whispered Bernard, wincing at the thought of adding 'squashed' to the list of the lemurs' ailments.

'I think I landed on one or two or maybe three or four...or,' she said, her voice barely audible above the chorus of screams and howls from the lemurs.

Bernard swept his binoculars across the platform below. The lemurs, who had been sitting and lying on their wooden tree house platform, were jumping around excitedly. The two dancing lemurs came into view, their arms held up to the sky as they danced across the enclosure in fright.

'So much for our covert operation,' muttered Bernard, focusing his torch beam on Larold. 'Here take this,' he added throwing a walkie-talkie down. 'And these for a distraction.'

Two bananas followed, each hitting the floor with a splat. Bernard watched her scramble around the floor for the bananas and the walkie-talkie along with a growing group of lemurs who were leaping down from above. She managed to grab one of the bananas and the walkie-talkie before a lemur jumped on her head, its thick black and white striped, mostly bald, tail swishing in front of her face.

'Ahhh...yuk! Get off me!'

It snatched the banana from her and jumped back to the platform and Larold, now unmolested, was free to creep towards the toilets. After a few minutes, the lemurs quietened down and settled themselves back to sleep.

Bernard was just refocusing the binoculars, when he heard a faint squeaking in the distance. He panned the binoculars over the enclosure, wondering if it was coming from an awake lemur playing on a swing tyre. But, as far as he could see, they were all snuggled up to each other, falling asleep once again. He listened carefully. The squeaking was getting louder and, as he desperately tried to work out where the noise was coming from, he glimpsed a flash of something moving along the train track in the distance, making its way towards the station.

'Too quiet for a train,' he said to himself.

He blinked several times until the shape suddenly took form. It was an old fashioned handcar being powered along the track by a shadowy undefined figure wearing what looked like a gigantic flowing cloak. Then Bernard lost sight of the handcar as it disappeared behind a clump of trees.

He scrambled to his feet and swept the binoculars up and down the track, desperate to locate the mysterious figure again. But when he focused on the station, he saw the handcar parked next to a train. The mysterious figure had vanished.

Bernard gulped and grabbed his walkie-talkie, pressing down the button to speak.

'The phantom fur shaver has landed! I repeat the fur shaver has landed! Over!'

'What?' said Bernard as his own voice was broadcast through the other walkie-talkie from below. 'Come in, Larold. Over!' he tried again.

But again his voice came back at him loud and clear.

'I bet she's forgotten how to use it,' he muttered. 'Larold. Press the button down when you speak,' said Bernard, who nearly fell out of the tree as his walkie-talkie emitted a terrible scream.

The noise was followed by what sounded like fumbling as if someone had grabbed the walkie-talkie and was trying to work out how to use it.

'Larold? Are you okay? Come in, Larold!'

Again the walkie-talkie threw out a terrible squealing but this time Bernard recognised it. He trailed his binoculars on the lemurs below and saw two of them fighting over it.

However, there was no time to retrieve it because out of the corner of his eye, Bernard saw a cloak-wearing shadow flit across the enclosure. He took his binoculars and with shaky hands, zoomed in on the hooded figure as it drew closer, now appearing like a cross between Dracula and a deranged-looking monk.

'Larold, please don't come back now. Please,' he gasped as he observed the supernatural figure with ever widening eyes.

It seemed to move in an odd though fluid way as if its body was made of two or three separate parts, one part moving in one direction, another slipping along in the opposite direction before moving again in yet another direction, all the while shrouded in a monstrous hooded cape.

Bernard gulped again as he tried to imagine himself wrestling the beast to the ground to attach the tracker. It was nearly upon the tree now and Bernard frantically zoomed the lens closer with shaky hands, taking in its hideous form, a mass of dark flesh, covered in little patches of fur and beards of yellow.

'Hang on,' said Bernard. 'I've seen those beards before. It is the same beast from the garden. I knew it,' he said, holding the binoculars in one hand and rummaging in the rucksack with his other. 'They're going to have to believe me now.'

He pulled out the gun, freeing it from its t-shirt case, all the time watching the figure stoop down and empty the contents of a large pouch onto the floor.

'A pouch? Kangaroos have pouches but this is no kangaroo!' whispered Bernard as he witnessed dozens of bottles, bananas and apples tumbling to the ground.

As if in some kind of trance, the lemurs fell from the surrounding trees like the autumn leaves and scurried over to the creature, its many hands working quickly together in a blurred frenzy, handing out the bottles to the lemurs, who happily guzzled down the liquid inside.

Bernard suddenly became aware of the weight of gun in his hand and the fact that he'd never fired one before in his life. It can't be that hard, he'd reasoned when he retrieved it from the safe. At least the figure was large. He couldn't possibly miss something that big. He took aim and squeezed the trigger peering down at the beast, determined to be courageous. He thought of his mother and father, who had stared down lions and tigers in the wild, and had wrestled anacondas and crocodiles. He heard their voices in his head: 'Stay calm, Bernard, love, and fire before it's too late.'

But just as he did so, he heard a rustling from above and momentarily looked up to see a lemur about to leap on him.

Bernard swerved just as the gun went off, the dart shooting into the darkness below followed by a yelp and a loud thud.

'Yes! Got you, whoever you are,' he shouted, quickly climbing to the platform below and leaping to the ground.

But, as he landed, he stumbled backwards at the sight before him. The creature seemed to rise like a spectre and float across the enclosure towards the fence. Bernard shakily reloaded the gun, realising it was his last chance to halt the beast in its tracks.

'Stop right there!' he demanded and fired the gun again as the creature scaled the two wooden fences before coming to a sudden stop at the outer barbed wire fence.

'Aha! Got you!' said Bernard, racing towards it.

However, as he drew closer, he could see that the beast was anything but tranquillised.

It was thrashing around wildly trying to free itself from the barbed wire fence. He cringed as he heard a loud ripping, imagining the terrible pain the creature must be suffering in its desperate attempt to escape. I have to help it, thought Bernard as he reached the fence but as he did so, a sickening tearing sound echoed across the zoo, making Bernard's knees turn to jelly.

Bernard crept closer to see all that remained of the beast were huge chunks of its exotic fur tangled in the barbed wire. He quickly grabbed his night vision binoculars and scanned the field leading to the station.

'Poor, poor creature,' said Bernard, feeling guilty for cornering it and causing it to tear itself open on the barbed wire.

That's until he caught sight of three very familiar shapes scampering towards the handcar on the railway track.

'Emile, Zola, Titus! I'm going to kill you!' shouted Bernard, giving chase before tripping over several discarded bottles of *Dr Wu's Sleepy Sleepy Now* potion and landing next to a snoring Larold.

Chapter 30

'Is she going to be all right?'

Bernard shone the torch over Larold's sleeping body to show Sarah-Jane where he'd accidently shot Larold with the tranquilliser dart.

'She'll be fine,' answered Sarah-Jane. 'But these tranquillisers are meant for large animals like elephants, and rhinos so she could be asleep until later today or even tomorrow morning.'

Bernard had tried to shake Larold awake but she was as fast asleep as the lemurs who'd guzzled down the bottles of *Dr Wu's Sleepy Sleepy Now*, their little bald bodies littering their enclosure. He remembered Sara-Jane's kind offer to call her anytime, day or night, and so had rang her straight away.

'Though it was a good shot, Bernard,' said Sarah-Jane, yanking the dart out of Larold's buttock. 'Just a shame you got the wrong target. Any sign of Emile, Zola or Titus?'

'No. But wait until I get hold of them.'

Bernard could no longer bury his head in the sand about their behaviour. The evidence was overwhelming. Not only had Bernard seen them running towards the station, but while waiting for Sarah-Jane to arrive, he'd examined the chunks of fur attached to the barbed wire: bits of the zoo animals' fur stuck to his father's old rain cape with superglue.

After putting Larold to bed, Bernard searched the house for the monkeys. But they were nowhere to be seen. However, Bernard knew they'd be back when they were hungry. That they were hiding away like they always did when in trouble.

Bernard was too cross with the monkeys to sleep. Instead, he stayed up for the rest of the night devising a series of punishments for them, including no asparagus for a month, no sweets for six weeks and no computer games for six months. But their main punishment, he decided, would be to clean and paint the old warthog enclosure. When he'd taken over the zoo, he'd moved the warthogs into Armando's enclosure as it was in better condition. But the warthogs had recently had triplets and their growing family needed more space and they were to move back to their former home in a couple of days. And Bernard would make sure the monkeys helped. If they misbehaved, the warthogs, notoriously bad-tempered and bossy, would keep an eye out on them. If they displayed even the slightest hint of bad behaviour, they'd be on hand to sort them out.

As soon as the sun rose, Bernard crept to the playhouse to check if the monkeys had sneaked back during the night. But there was no sign they'd slept there.

He set about searching through every nook and cranny and came away with further damning evidence. Stuffed between planks of wood and concealed in their tyre swings, Bernard discovered several dozen biscuit tins full of the missing fur. He piled the evidence high in a wheelbarrow and took it back to the house, wondering if there was a way he could offer the animals their fur back - minus the biscuit crumbs - and perhaps glue it on until their hair re-grew.

In terms of punishing the monkeys, there was nothing he could do but wait. In the meantime, he realised there was something very important he could no longer put off. He had to check the contents of the folder Larold had left on his desk. It was the least he could do after mistakenly shooting her.

So after checking on Larold, who showed no signs of waking up any time soon, he went into his office and took the folder from the drawer.

'There's no easy way to do this,' he said, closing his eyes, then turning around a large silver photo frame on the mantelpiece to face him.

He opened his eyes to see it was a photo of himself as a toddler, holding a bucket and spade with his mum on nearby Sunny Sands. He wiped the dust away from the glass, staring at his mother. He'd forgotten how pretty she was with her long dark hair and bright blue eyes, the very same eyes he found difficult to meet whenever he looked in a mirror. He grabbed another photo frame, this time it was of him and his father, again he was a toddler, sitting on his father's lap in a restaurant.

A whisper of a memory swirled around him as he recalled the heat and the sweet smell of fresh mangos and pineapple. He turned the largest of all the photo frames. It was his parents on their wedding day, huge grins bursting across their faces and Bernard couldn't help smiling too. It didn't seem possible that two people so beautiful and so young, could be dead.

'I'm so sorry,' said Bernard touching his parents' faces, willing them to materialise.

He took the first newspaper article out from the folder Larold had left and began to read. It was an obituary from *The Sunday Planet*.

The sudden deaths of Suki and Bernard Bamuel has left the world of conservation in mourning.

They were two of the most famous and outspoken campaigners against the practice of so-called trophy hunting in areas of Africa where tourists are allowed to shoot lions, wild elephants, zebras, giraffes, cheetahs, leopards, rhinos and hippos in areas for 'fun' in the name of conservation.

They repeatedly called for the practice to be banned, arguing it is not only cruel and senseless, but that many of the animals hunted are endangered and that only a small percentage of the fees paid go into conservation.

The tireless campaigners had also railed against canned hunting, poaching and the illicit trade of endangered species animal parts for use in quack medicine for many years. They were said to be close to devising a tracking device for elephants and rhinos which would help rangers identify and prosecute poachers more easily.

Both were also outspoken against cruelty to animals closer to home, questioning the need for factory farming to produce meat and milk, as well as fur farming.

Professor Luke Harvey of the famous Zoological Institute said that the world would be a poorer place without the Bamuels.

'They were two of the most powerful animal rights' activists in the world who managed to raise awareness of the issues of

poaching and trophy hunting in a world that is often blind to the savagery visited upon animals, especially endangered species. Unfortunately, in doing so, they made many enemies, some of whom will no doubt be celebrating their premature demise,' he said.

Suki and Bernard had met at the University of Birmingham's undergraduate zoology degree, and married soon after graduating. They leave behind their only son, Bernard.

An inquest has opened into their deaths.

As he re-read the words, it felt like he'd been reading about two strangers, not his parents. They were such good, brave people who had devoted their lives to animals. Yet how had they managed to spawn someone as horrid and cowardly as him? wondered Bernard.

He took out the next sheet of paper with shaky hands. It was the report into the inquest that Ms Snodgeweed had refused to let him attend, saying it would be too upsetting. Through a blur of tears, he began to read.

Mystery over popular naturalists' deaths in Zambia

An open verdict had been returned on the deaths of famous naturalists Suki and Bernard Bamuel when their hot air balloon burst into flames, killing them both instantly.

The pair had been holidaying in the national safari park with their 8-year-old son Bernard at the time, who was reportedly too ill to go on the balloon trip.

The coroner brought to light police evidence showing three bullet holes found in the remains of the basket which the balloon operators say were not present before take off.

'Bullet holes?' said Bernard, springing from his seat.

He paced the room, re-reading the paragraph urgently

again and again, the words striking at him like blows. He felt his legs wobble and quickly sat down at the desk before gobbling up the rest of the words.

Witnesses said several shots had been heard just before the balloon exploded, though no official hunting was taking place in the park and there were no reports of poachers in the area.

Bernard closed his eyes and willed himself back to that fateful day. He'd spent years trying to block out events but however hard he tried, they were as fresh in his mind as if it'd happened yesterday. How he'd clambered out and fallen to the ground, watching the basket tilting over, his parents desperately hanging onto the side as his mother screamed and his father yelled at him.

His eyes snapped open as he recalled something else. Among all the chaos, he had heard several shots as he watched the balloon right itself and then fly higher and higher. The shooting had stopped for several moments and then started again, spooking a flock of birds. But because Bernard always blamed himself, he'd never connected the two events.

He stood and walked across to the window, noticing a sudden lightness to his step. And as he gazed out across the fields, he allowed himself to think for just a split second that he hadn't been to blame for his parents' deaths after all. But, as he walked back to sit at the desk once again, he felt a familiar heaviness return.

'If I wasn't to blame, who was?'

He grabbed the report and read on.

The Coroner Ms Katherine Martello called tourist Rupert Yeno-Mevoli to give evidence after he witnessed the balloon exploding above him. Though several witnesses reported hearing

shots being fired at the time of the accident, Mr Yeno-Mevoli,
who was on his honeymoon at the time, said he didn't remember
hearing any.

He told the Coroner: 'I don't know anything about any shoot-
ing or guns. I was too busy staring into the eyes of my beautiful
bride. All I know is that the balloon was in the air one minute
and zooming to the ground the next. To be honest the whole
episode ruined our honeymoon.'

In summing up, Ms Martello said: 'Though there are
clearly many question marks over what happened on that fate-
ful day, I am left with no option but to record an open verdict.
If more evidence should arise in the future, then the inquest will
be reopened.'

Bernard read the report several times, stumbling over the
words of the witness statement: *To be honest, the whole episode*
ruined our honeymoon.

'Funnily enough, it ruined my whole life,' spat Bernard.
'And why call their deaths an 'episode'? What a cheek! It
makes it sound as if it was something from *Bouffant Bay*. Not
real life.'

But it was real. It was his life. His parents' lives. They'd
been taken from him in their prime.

Bernard lost track of time as he retrieved a photo he kept
at the back of a drawer. It'd been taken in the garden during
a heavy snowfall a few months before his parents' deaths. His
arms were flung around a lopsided snowman while his mother
had her arms around him and, he remembered how his father
had done his usual dashing back from setting up the photo,
just in time to have the top of his head in the photo. He

started at the photo, imagining all the possible scenarios of that fateful day.

That a poacher had accidently fired several bullets into the balloon's gas canister. Though you could explain one shot but not three, surely?

And then an even darker, more upsetting thought came to Bernard. Why would someone be shooting in the air? Lions, rhinos and elephants didn't fly as far as he was aware, so were the shots deliberate?

He knew his parents had made many enemies. And, as he allowed himself to think of them again, waves of distant memories, he'd managed to hold back for the last four years, crashed over him one at a time.

There was one in particular which was so vivid it felt like it'd just happened. He must have been five or six and he'd run to the door to collect a parcel from the postman and sat in the kitchen watching his mother unwrap the brown paper, the colour draining from her face as she opened up a cardboard box to find a rat's severed head inside. Bernard had been struck by its greasy hair and the length of its whiskers and how cross it had looked at having been decapitated and stuck in a box.

Then there had been a series of anonymous letters threatening to kill them for carrying on with their campaigns against big game hunters. And how the police had come round several times, his parents closing the kitchen door behind them, telling him to go to his room or to play outside. Though he always stayed outside listening at the door, trying to catch snatches of their heated but hushed conversations.

Then the numerous times he'd pick up the phone to hear

steady breathing down the other end and sometimes nothing but silence until the line went dead.

And the ginger-bearded man with bad breath who'd been waiting for him outside Fluffingdale Primary School gates, saying his parents had sent him to pick him up. He'd driven off quickly when the head teacher had confronted him.

He remembered the smell of his mother's apple shampoo as she smothered him with his kisses, telling him she would keep him safe from now on. That's why he'd been sent to boarding school. They wanted him to be safe. They tried to say it was because they were travelling so much.

But Bernard now remembered the real reason. People who wanted to do bad things to animals, wanted to do bad things to his parents and to him.

Then a terrible thought struck Bernard, sending such a chill down his spine that he wondered if the snowman had reached out of the photo with a big icy finger and touched him. And that thought was this; someone had murdered his parents.

Chapter 31

'I don't like to say but...' said Larold as soon as she woke up that evening.

'I told you so,' said Bernard, finishing off her sentence.

He didn't mind being proved wrong. He was just relieved that Larold didn't have any bad side effects from being tranquillised. Bernard had spent the afternoon by her bedside, waiting for her to wake, mulling over where he'd gone wrong with the monkeys. He realised everyone in the whole world could see they were badly behaved apart from him, although deep down he'd known they were. He just hadn't known what to do about it. And now he felt particularly foolish.

Flashbacks of their bad behaviour crowded around him as he recalled how they regularly trashed the kitchen looking for their favourite snacks. Not to mention the time he'd found all his cuddly toys nailed to the playroom walls, a particularly upsetting event, followed by their eventual gutting and turning into handbags and rugs.

But worries about his rubbish parenting were nothing compared to the dark shadow looming over him. Someone had killed his parents and got away with it.

At first, he felt numb, as if someone had sucked out all his emotions. Then little spikes of anger stabbed at him as he wondered how anyone could do such a terrible thing, to take another's life. What kind of person would murder such good people? wondered Bernard. Someone who wanted to silence them, came the resounding answer.

He remembered how outspoken his parents had been against trophy hunters, poachers, the makers and users of quack medicine, as well as the practice of factory farming and fur farming. And there was one thing they repeated again and again. Stand up for what you believe in, and never be a by-stander, no matter if someone laughs at you, or threatens you. Because they will laugh and they will try to silence you with either words and threats. But you have to do the right thing.

And now it was his turn to do the right thing and discover the truth.

'And you were right about my parents' deaths,' said Bernard.

'You've been blaming yourself, haven't you?' said Larold, sitting up to take a sip of the hot tea Bernard had just made her.

Bernard nodded and looked down at his feet, feeling himself blushing furiously as he made his confession.

'I..I...jumped out of the balloon, you see, just as it took off. I was terrified of heights and too scared to tell them. They were such adventurers, so brave. I felt useless compared to them. I didn't want to disappoint them. They are...they *were* famous for standing up for animals and there was me, their cowardly son.'

'So, you leapt out?'

Bernard nodded, unable to meet Larold's eyes.

'There's nothing wrong with being frightened of things,

especially heights and...and... you're not a coward,' she said, touching him gently on his shoulder. 'You stood up to that horrible man and saved all the zoo animals. I think you're wonderful,' she said. 'Even if you did shoot me.'

Bernard felt the blush erupting once again.

'Don't worry, you're not that wonderful,' said Larold, pushing him gently on the shoulder. 'But you know now it was nothing to do with you. You can't blame yourself. It's obvious someone shot at their balloon. And thank god you'd jumped off, or else you wouldn't be here today,' she added, patting Bernard's shoulder.

'I've always felt I don't deserve to be here. I've always wished I could travel back in time and swap places with them.'

'No, they loved you, Bernard. They would have hated to see you blaming yourself.'

Bernard took the crumpled inquest report from his pocket and handed it to Larold.

'I can't stop thinking about what that Rupert whatever his name is, the witness, said about my parents' deaths ruining his honeymoon.'

'Horrible man,' said Larold, scanning the report. 'And isn't it strange how he protests a little too much about not hearing shots? Are you okay?' she asked, realising he'd gone quiet.

Bernard looked up. Through his tears, Larold could see a strength burning in his eyes she'd not seen before.

'He's either deaf or lying. I remember hearing shooting. You couldn't not hear it.'

Bernard turned his face from Larold. Now that he was

talking to someone about his parents being murdered, it all seemed too overwhelming.

'Hey, you know what? Your parents may be dead but you were lucky to have such a cool mum and dad for eight years of your life. I wish my parents were even a tiny little bit as brave as yours.'

'I'd rather have living ones...' he trailed off, guessing that Larold often wondered if her mum was still alive.

'In that obituary, the professor says they were always getting death threats. Can you remember them?'

'Yes, a few. They always creeped me out, written using cut out letters. Mum and Dad always hid them out of sight.'

'Did your parents ever say if they had suspicions as to who these people were?'

'No, take your pick from the world, they used to say. The trade in illegal animal parts is worth something stupid like £17 billion a year. More than drugs. I remember Mum saying rhino horn was worth more than gold. It's difficult to know where to start.'

'Let's make a list of all those who have a motive,' said Larold, grabbing a pen and notebook from her bedside table.

'The likes of Dr Wu for start and then people who like hunting animals. Also the so-called 'canned hunters'.'

'Those are the farms that breed lions for shooting?'

Bernard nodded.

Larold scrunched up her face as if in pain. 'What kind of person wants to shoot them in the first place?'

'The kind of person who posts photos of themselves posing with a gun and a dead lion on social media to show off to their friends.'

'That's so messed up.'

'Very,' agreed Bernard. 'Anyway, what I do remember is the letters increased when they were interviewed for a newspaper article, revealing they were close to developing the tracking device.'

'To stop poachers and big game trophy hunters?'

'Mostly to stop poachers but yes, also the trophy hunters who were getting away with shooting the animals by buying people's silence. They were worried because, although the technology was in its early stages, in terms of placing the device on an animal and having connectivity...'

'Internet access?'

'Yes, which can be nearly impossible in remote areas of Africa. But they were getting close. They even had a satellite company all lined up to provide free coverage...' said Bernard, recalling the day when his parents had returned from a trip to London where they'd had talks with the satellite operators.

'Did they keep any of the death threats?'

'I guess they must have handed them over to the police.'

'All of them?'

Bernard cast his mind back. He remembered his father getting cross with him one day after he'd been poking around in the office looking for a pack of cards his mum had sent him to fetch. She'd told him they were in the bureau and he'd just opened it, when he felt his hand being smacked away but not before Bernard had spotted a bundle of letters.

'I'm not sure,' said Bernard.

'Well, let's go and have a look,' she said, discarding the list of suspects and throwing the duvet off her.

But as they made their way downstairs, they heard the sound of wheels crunching on the gravel.

'Looks like we have visitors,' he said running to the window and peering out.

They watched as Ryan's beaten up old Land Rover came to a halt, Bob in the back circling what looked like a lifeless mound of sacking.

'Oh, please, no!' said Bernard, putting his hand over his mouth, fearing the worst.

He sprinted down the stairs, Larold calling for him to wait. Ryan was unbolting the back of the Land Rover when he flew through the door.

'They're not...not...dead, are they?' stuttered Bernard, running towards him.

'Don't be soft. They're hiding. Bob found them cowering in the cowshed,' said Ryan. 'Frightened, no doubt, of what you'll do to punish them, if you've got any sense.'

Chapter 32

Two days after solving the mystery of the missing fur, Bernard set the monkeys to work in the warthog enclosure for three hours a day before their afternoon performance. They were to paint the railings and the wooden shelter white. But first they had the unpleasant task of hosing down the old outdoor living quarters and the warthog's feeding troughs to make them look as good as new.

Bernard stayed for an hour or so supervising their tasks and was pleased to see the monkeys were terrified of the family of six warthogs, who would trot over and sniff them with their rough bristly noses whenever the monkeys started to slacken, which was pretty often.

Meanwhile, Bernard took a rare afternoon off and went home, while Loki and Armando stayed with Larold and the tigers for the rest of the day. His memory of the death threat letters had kept niggling at him ever since talking to Larold. They hadn't had a chance to look for them once the monkeys had returned home and then the following morning, it was back to work at the zoo. He kept remembering the stinging feeling of his hand being slapped away by his father, telling him to keep out of the office.

Perhaps the letters were still there? Maybe the police had

missed some crucial evidence, something obvious they'd over-looked that Bernard would spot instead?

Back in his office, he walked towards the large bureau. His grandfather's portrait loomed particularly large today. It was staring down at him as if to say: *You know you were banned from going anywhere near the bureau, Bernard.* And now as he opened it up, he realised why.

In one corner was a bundle of old black and white photos held together by a thick rubber band. He took it off and sifted through just a few of them, wincing. They were photos of elephants and rhinos, dead with their tusks and horns severed and missing, the scrappy African grass stained dark red around them.

He searched through a pile of paperwork. It was mostly receipts for flights and taxis dating from up to ten years ago. He opened a small drawer on the left, jammed with packs of cards, and then another on the right where he found a bundle of letters. Bernard pulled them out.

'Bingo!'

They were written on a typewriter in a mixture of capital and lower case letters while two were written using letters cut out from magazines and newspapers.

They were all on the same theme and all anonymous. He read through them, feeling more and more nauseous.

'DOGodERS DiE.'

'yoU DESERVE to die like VERMIN.'

'NO RUINING OUR GAME. LEAVE AFRICA 4 TRUE ANIMAL LOVERS.'

He held each letter up to the sunlight streaming through the window, desperately searching for some clue, any clue at all. But the senders had been careful. The paper was plain white office paper. The cut out letters were standard fonts used by numerous newspapers and magazines all over the world.

Of course, there would be no clues. What was he expecting? A giant cross saying 'Murderer's DNA here'. Who was he kidding, thinking a 12-year-old boy could solve a mystery the police and his parents hadn't been able to?

Bernard carefully placed them back into the bureau and locked it, angry tears falling. Whoever had killed them had got away with it, probably forever. Bernard glanced at the photo of his parent's wedding day on the mantelpiece. They'd got married in Zambia where they'd had their honeymoon too, just like the horrible witness at the inquest whose insensitive words were etched in his brain forever.

'*To be honest the whole episode ruined our honeymoon.*'

'What was his name again?' Bernard asked the photo of his parents.

He'd meant to search for it on the internet when he'd first read the inquest but he'd been distracted by the monkeys going missing. He took out the crumpled inquest report from his pocket, scanned it quickly until he found the name *Rupert Yeno-Mevoli*, opened up his laptop and typed in the name into a search engine.

Immediately, dozens of posts from celebrity and society magazines like *Minted* and *Tally-Ho!* popped up. Bernard clicked onto one dated from 2006 and began reading.

Ladies will be weeping into their Pimms as Tally-Ho's! Third Most Eligible Bachelor 2005, Rupert 'heartthrob' Yeno-Mevoli ties the knot with Lady Bushcutter-Smythe, only child of the recently deceased billionaire banker, Lord Bushcutter-Smythe.

Bernard found himself lurching backwards as a picture of an unattractive boss-eyed man in his twenties grinning inanely at a pretty red-haired girl came into view.

Eeek! *Tally-Ho!* can't have had many bachelors to choose from, thought Bernard.

He clicked on the next post from *Minted*. It was an exclusive interview with Rupert talking about the tragic death of his wife in a car accident just a year after their wedding.

Rupert tells Minted how he managed to crawl out of the wreckage of the crash that killed his young wife, Lady Bushcutter-Smythe, and how he'll never love again.

Bernard clicked on the next post.

'Never love again!' exclaimed Bernard, taking in the photo of Rupert getting married 18 months later.

Tragic widower Rupert tells Tally-Ho! how he found love with heir to the Arc Helicopter Empire, Sacha Primose, and how it has healed his broken heart.

'Bet it has!' said Bernard, gazing at the photos of Rupert and his new bride at their palatial mansion in America.

The next post was from *The Daily Celeb* three years later with a photo of Rupert getting married yet again.

'He's a serial...marrier,' said Bernard. 'And very unlucky with his wives or more to the point, they're very unlucky around him.'

Third time lucky for tragic twice-widowed Rupert as he marries the queen of toothpaste Trudy Shine in her beachside Malibu mansion. Rupert shares his heartbreak with Minted over second wife's tragic fall from helicopter.

He carried on clicking through all the articles, counting five marriages in total, including to Lady Annabel Bungley-Binglington who he was on honeymoon with when his parents were killed. Up to this point most of the photos were taken by paparazzi on long lenses, and only one was a close up. Bernard leant into the screen examining his face. He always wore a top hat which meant most of his features were hidden in shadow but still there was something very familiar about him. It was something about his mouth, realised Bernard comparing the photos of him. It was the way that the corners turned down even when he was smiling.

As he scrolled down onto the next page, his eye caught the name of an animal protection organisation and he clicked on the post.

Save the Animals is increasingly worried about the growing trend of trophy hunting in Africa and the lack of data being kept about the number of animals being killed. After approaching several reservations in Africa, we were unable to obtain any numbers for how many people visit the reserves to shoot animals and how many lions, zebras, rhinos and elephants have been shot. However, thanks to our supporters, we've been able to compile a list of the worst offenders.

Bernard scanned through the list of names and suddenly gripped the desk as he came across a very familiar name there in black and white.

Baron Von Hesti previously known as Rupert Yeno-Mevoli.

Bernard re-read the line over and over again, feeling as if the whole world was shifting beneath him.

'What? They're the same person?' he said, trying to make sense of it all.

He quickly typed in the name Baron Von Hesti and an article in *Minted* showed him posing with a dead giraffe and holding up a huge bloodied organ. Bernard scanned the picture caption.

Baron Von Hesti's unusual Valentine's gift.

'What the hell?' said Bernard, unable to believe his eyes as he read on.

'I always wanted to shoot a giraffe and what better Valentine's gift from my true love than providing me with a present to shoot one and cut out a real heart. Perfecto!' said the Baron.

'You monster!' spat Bernard, quickly clicking off the upsetting image.

The next article to come up was from *Hunting, Shooting 'n' Killing Monthly*, penned by none other than blood-thirsty Baron Von Hesti, telling readers why trophy hunting was good for conservation. As Bernard read the first paragraph it felt as though someone had gripped him by the ankles, tipped him upside and was shaking him violently.

'Certain well-known do-gooders say trophy hunting has no place in conservation. I even hear that they're trying out a tracking device against poachers. It will never work. You will need uninterrupted internet connection and how on earth are you going to tag the animals? Ask them nicely to hold out a paw while you fit the damn thing?! Even if the former was possible, how are the gamekeepers going to reach the poachers in time?'

Bernard thought back on the nasty anonymous letters. 'Do-gooders' was a word that was often used. He read on.

'A far better way is to allow trophy hunting and so-called canned hunting to expand. This way, the money raised by the

increased number of fees will pay for more workers to patrol the land against poachers and we can have our fun too!!!

'It's a win-win situation for everyone, and yes, including the animals, because we're saving them from being butchered by poachers, who often leave the animals bleeding to death after cutting off their tusks and horns whereas we just shoot them to death.

'People need to learn that these animals aren't the furry little cuddly toys we buy for children. They have vicious claws, teeth and tusks. They're nasty beasts with no feelings other than where to find their next feast. If they have their way they will get trophy hunting banned in all the countries where we shoot big game. Someone needs to stop these do-gooders from ruining our fun before it's too late.'

'And was that someone you, Von Hesti?' shouted Bernard as he felt a violent rage surging through him. 'That's why you were so keen to give me the zoo. It wasn't because of the monkeys. When I called you a murderer, you thought I was talking about my parents, didn't you? You killed them and then thought you could buy me off!'

Bernard went to pick up the phone to call the police but before he dialled the last digit, he slammed it back down.

What was the point? He could tell them and they may well believe him. But there was one crucial thing missing: evidence.

'There must be something?' He turned back to the computer and looked up flights for Zambia. Perhaps he could go back and ask the police to reopen their investigation? There must be some residue left from the gun powder on the balloon, thought Bernard. Perhaps they could trace it back to a weapon Von Hesti had owned?

Then Bernard remembered the newspaper report. The few remains of the basket had gone up in flames in a mysterious fire at the local police station therefore destroying any evidence linking Von Hesti to the shooting, realised Bernard, letting the angry tears roll down his cheeks.

Chapter 33

Bernard arrived back at the zoo in such a turmoil he didn't notice the large crowd gathered outside the warthog enclosure.

Much to the visitors' amusement, Emile, Zola and Titus were being chased from one end to the other by the family of warthogs.

Indeed, it was only ten minutes later, when he retraced his steps after failing to find Larold and Brenda that he happened to glance over and see the throng moving their heads from side to side as if watching a tennis match whilst jeering and laughing.

'What's going on?' he asked no-one in particular because deep down he knew exactly what was going on; the monkeys had been misbehaving and the warthogs' patience had finally run out.

Bernard politely made his way through the crowds until he came to the entrance of the warthog enclosure. Both the monkeys and the warthogs skidded to a halt as soon as they saw him standing there, a scowl that could curdle milk etched across his face.

'I can't leave you for five minutes without you messing everything up,' he shouted.

Emile, Zola and Titus looked up at Bernard and shook their heads, pointing over at the warthogs, who trotted back towards their feeding troughs.

'You can't blame them. They're here to discipline you,' scolded Bernard.

He watched the warthogs make a great show of wandering near to the troughs, throw their snouts in the air and squeal loudly as if they'd taken in a whiff of mouldy cheese before running to the water trough and dunking their noses in as if trying to wash away the smell.

'Please tell me you haven't been feeding them anything nasty? Not more of Dr Wu's evil potions?' asked Bernard, despairing of their naughtiness.

The monkeys shook their heads in denial once again and pulled at his sleeves, wildly gesticulating for him to go to the long line of feeding troughs they were supposed to be cleaning out.

Bernard marched to the troughs, the monkeys following behind, careful not to get too close to the warthogs. He looked down and a mush of putrid brown goo stared back, emitting a rotten cabbage, Brussel sprout and egg stink which nearly knocked them all off their feet.

Bernard staggered backwards. He then took off his sweatshirt and tied it around his face like a mask and grabbed a twig to unblock the drain but there was too much gunk and it snapped easily.

He'd need something far stronger.

'Fetch me a spade, please,' he said to Titus.

Titus obediently jumped over the railings into the tool

shed and scampered back with one, followed by Larold, Ryan and Brenda trailing behind.

'I've been searching for you everywhere,' said Bernard, looking up as his friends joined him. 'Is everything all right?' he asked Ryan, who wasn't, as a rule, a regular visitor to the zoo.

'Oh yes, all fine,' said Brenda. 'Ryan popped over to ask me for dinner,' she added, a huge smile spreading across her face while a blush spread across Ryan's.

'Oh, right,' said Bernard, catching Larold's eye and grinning.

'What's going on? We were having lunch and then saw all the crowds gathering,' asked Larold.

'For once it's actually not the monkeys' faults. The feeding troughs are in a worse state than I thought. I don't think they've ever been cleaned,' explained Bernard.

'They really do stink,' said Larold, wafting away the turgid smell with her hands. 'Is that why you were looking for us? Did you want some help?'

'No, I've got something really important to tell you, but first I need to sort this out,' said Bernard. He grabbed the spade from Titus and began scraping and digging away the compacted gunk until he reached the bottom of one of the troughs.

'Looks like the drain's blocked,' said Larold, from a safe distance.

'Yes, definitely blocked,' said Ryan, peeking over Larold's shoulder.

'Most certainly blocked,' added Brenda.

'Yes, I DO KNOW,' exploded Bernard.

'We're just saying,' said Larold, taken aback by Bernard's ill temper.

'Well, if you're so interested, you can all give me a hand. We need to pull the pipe off,' he said, kneeling under the trough, resigning himself to getting filthy.

Larold held her breath and squatted next to Bernard on one side while Brenda and Ryan grabbed the other side of the pipe.

'One, two, three and...'

With one massive tug the pipe came away, throwing them off balance to the muddy ground and setting the warthogs off into a squealing frenzy as they darted to the far edge of their enclosure. The monkeys, standing away from the stink, tried to hide their giggles behind their hands.

'Don't you dare,' warned Ryan, helping Brenda up.

After brushing themselves down, they examined the pipe carefully.

'Full of crisp packets and sweet wrappers. Disgusting,' said Brenda.

'Throw that one away and I'll fix up a new one,' offered Ryan.

'Hold on a minute,' said Larold, disappearing into the shed and returning with a toolbox. 'Try and ease whatever's blocking it out with this,' she said, handing him a screwdriver.

'It won't work,' said Bernard, trying and failing to keep the irritation out of his voice.

'Let me have a go,' said Larold, who carried on trying to push and dig the mush out.

But it was solid. Nothing could budge it.

'There's only thing for it,' Bernard said, determined to see what was blocking the pipe, now he'd invested so much time and effort into it.

'Stand back,' he added as he smashed the plastic pipe against the wall of the feeding store. After several attempts, the pipe eventually fractured and a compacted tube of mud, mixed with different coloured paper, dropped to the floor.

'Look at all those wrappers. I mean it's not as if there aren't loads of bins here,' complained Brenda.

Larold tried to scoop it up with a spade. But the tube of rubbish rolled off, landing at Bernard's feet. Larold was just about to slice it in half with the spade when Bernard grabbed it from her.

'Hang on a moment. Look!' he said, pointing at some scrawly writing in blue ink.

'Just a load of rubbish,' said Brenda. 'Give it here and I'll chuck it in the bin on the way back to the shop.'

Bernard squatted down to get a closer look.

'It looks as if there's some kind of letter in there,' said Larold.

They glanced at one another, puzzled as to why the warthogs had started up their squealing frenzy once again and Bernard began to unwrap the bundle, discarding the sweet wrappers, until the neat handwriting was now clear enough to read.

'...destroy... this... letter... as soon as you've read its contents,' he read out loud.

'Eh?' said Larold, peering at the note over his shoulder.

He carefully unfurled the rest of the wrappers revealing the whole note, slightly torn and ragged and the ink running in parts but still legible.

My darling Snuggaluffagus Rupert Bear,

I've ordered Dr Wu's Sleepy-Sleepy Forever to be delivered to your London flat.

You'll administer five drops of the potion in her tea on the afternoon of her birthday. It falls on a Monday when the zoo is closed and I've booked all the zookeepers on a one-day animal massage course to make sure there are no busybodies around.

You then need to tempt Bunny to take afternoon tea with her beloved tigers, requesting she keeps them in their cage. When she's dead, you need to hit her on the back of head to make it look like the tigers have mauled her a little, then put the tigers into the cage and call the police.

Perfecto! It will be a much cleaner job than those animal-loving interfering Bamuel freaks you despised so much. You may have to go to Bunny's inquest but it will be an open and shut case unlike theirs!!! It won't be long before I'll have the honour of becoming your seventh and last wife and the new Baroness Von Hesti!

Can't wait! TTFN Tiger!

Yours forever,

Your Cuddlitious Cuddle Bear Trixie.

'A much cleaner job than those animal-loving interfering Bamuel freaks you despised so much,' repeated Bernard in a daze.

Bernard re-read the note, desperately trying to take in the enormity of the confession, his mouth opening and closing, but no words would come.

He passed the note to Ryan. Brenda and Larold huddled around and scanned it quickly.

'Murderers!' said Ryan.

'Monsters!' exclaimed Brenda.

'Are you all right?' asked Larold.

'Yes, I think I'm fine,' said Bernard, wiping away a few stray tears as a smile began to form on his lips. 'More than fine. Don't you see? We've got the evidence now,' he said, taking Larold by the shoulders and hugging her, then Ryan and Brenda in turn.

'Er...what do you mean?' asked Larold, once he'd let go of her.

'Von Hesti is the same person as that Rupert, the witness at the inquest, and the very same Rupert this note is addressed to. I found out this morning when I went through the reports again and did the internet search on his name. That's why I was looking for you. I wanted to tell you what I'd discovered,' explained Bernard.

'What? So Bunny's husband, Baron Von Hesti, is the same person as Rupert Yeno-Mevoli?' said Larold.

'Yes! He obviously wanted to take her name so he could become a Baron. He was just after her title.'

'The devil!' said Brenda.

'I knew there was something fishy about him when he just handed the zoo over to you like that, Bernard, but I couldn't put my finger on it,' said Ryan.

'And that explains why he was hanging around the warthog enclosure the day they handed the zoo over,' said Bernard.

'What do you mean?' asked Larold.

'He told me he was saying farewell to the warthogs because they were his favourites – even though he was planning to shoot them. Now we know why. He was counting on them to destroy the evidence.'

'Why the warthogs?' asked Larold, feeling even more confused by the turn of events.

'Warthogs and pigs are supposed to eat anything and I mean anything,' explained Bernard, with a knowing raised eyebrow.

'What? I bet they wouldn't have gone near my school dinners,' said Larold. 'And anyway why not just burn the evidence?'

'Maybe he was getting some kind of strange kick out of feeding it to the animals Bunny loved so much,' said Brenda.

'Whatever the truth, it's time to call the police and bring your parents' murderers to justice at last,' said Ryan.

Chapter 34

Inspector Strangewish was a shortish fellow with wispy blond hair and an amazingly pudgy face which contorted into all sorts of expressions of shock and disgust as Bernard relayed the story of finding the damning evidence. As the investigating officer into Bernard's parents' deaths, he'd arrived soon after Ryan's call and now stood in front of the warthog enclosure and the large crowd of visitors.

'Well, Bernard. It's a commonly held belief that warthogs and pigs eat anything, and I mean anything,' said Inspector Strangewish, raising his eyebrows in the same knowing fashion as Bernard had done just half an hour earlier. 'But and it's a very important but,' he added mysteriously before turning to Bernard and asking: 'Can I take the note for a moment, please?'

Inspector Strangewish held the note up and waved it over the railings at the warthogs, who were happily sunbathing in a patch of late afternoon sunshine. The effect was immediate. The warthogs squealed and ran to the furthest corner as if a gang of their worst enemies had just turned up. The crowd took a collective intake of breath.

The Inspector turned back to Bernard, returning the note to him.

'They kept doing that as we got closer to finding the note,' said Bernard.

'Yes, they would do. You see what Von Hesti or Rupert Yeno-Mevoli and that Trixie-Pixie or whatever her name is, failed to realise is that warthogs refuse to touch notes confessing to despicable crimes.

'Warthogs gag on the ink of killers and choke on the weasel words of murderers, and, ladies and gentlemen, Emile, Zola, Titus, Loki, Armando and all you zoo animals, we have these warthogs here to thank for the survival of this letter 18 months after Bunny was murdered, and four years after your parents' deaths, Bernard.

'And young man, you have your eagle eyes to thank for spotting the note. Well done!'

Just then the Inspector's radio buzzed.

'Excuse me,' he said, stepping away to take the call.

After a moment, he turned to Bernard.

'They got 'em just in time. Baron Von Hesti and that Trixie-Pixie were boarding his private jet for Brazil. And from what you've told me young man, it sounds like Von Hesti may have bumped off all of his wives too. I'll be contacting the police in the US to pass on my suspicions but for now neither of them will be flying anywhere for a very long time.'

***

And, so my friends, the story of the not so mysterious mystery of the missing fur has come to an end.

Inspector Strangewish and his detectives rushed away to charge Von Hesti and Trixie-Pixie. The crowd drifted back to their tours. Brenda reopened the gift shop. Ryan and Bob returned to the farm. Emile, Zola and Titus went back to painting the warthog enclosure, and Larold ran off to break the good news to Mr Stripey and Marley that no-one could accuse them of being man-eating tigers ever again.

And Bernard?

Well, after a few moments, he looked round to see that everyone had gone. Even Armando and Loki were nowhere to be seen, having snuck off for an afternoon nap. He was all alone, although he realised for the first time in his life that he felt anything but. He had everything he needed in life including a new project to carry on his parents' work on developing the anti-poaching tracking device.

And, as he glanced up at the sky, for a split second, he swore he saw a hot air balloon flying overhead with two very familiar figures waving and smiling down at him before disappearing behind the fluffy white clouds.

Michele lives by the seaside with her three children and a bitey cat. She has lots of short stories published in anthologies and magazines, her short plays have been performed in various theatres in England and her first short comedy film, *The Beast of Romney Marsh,* is available on You Tube. Before training as a reporter, Michele studied ancient history and archaeology, worked in bars, restaurants, a toy shop (best job), a pizza factory (worst job if you get stuck on centring olives all day) and taught English in Brazil. *The Mystery of the Missing Fur (And Far More Mysterious Mysteries)* is Michele's second children's book. *The Stone of Surinam* was published in 2020 on Kindle. You can find her on Instagram @shelshelsheldon, Twitter @ShelshelMichele or at michelesheldon.com

Lightning Source UK Ltd.
Milton Keynes UK
UKHW010628270621
386200UK00001B/58

9 781838 465506